SITTIN' IN AMEN CORNER

David Coppage

Publisher's Name: David Coppage

ISBN: 978-1-968442-35-4

EBOOK ISBN: 978-1-968442-51-4

CONTENTS

ACKNOWLEDGMENTS

Thanks to my mom and dad, Frank and Jackie Coppage, for much of the inspiration that went into creating this story. To my best friend, Melissa, an awesome wife and mother, and to Casey and Kyle- the two best kids any father ever had. Special thanks as well to some dear people who read my raw manuscript and gave me much needed feedback that helped make this story what it became: Melanie Flora; Mike Rich; John Shirley; Jeni Coppage; Peggy Ryan.

CHAPTER ONE

Bless Your Lil' Heart

Tom Franks rested comfortably in his hospital bed, a ventilator attached to the intubation tube inserted in his airway, providing him with the life-sustaining oxygen he needed to maintain life. A myriad of wires emanating from beneath his hospital gown were connected to the monitor in his ICU room, indicating his heart rate and blood pressure were at tolerable levels and of no immediate concern. At ninety-three years of age and suffering from congestive heart failure, Tom was literally in the midst of his last breaths on earth.

His beloved daughter, Karen, whom Tom described a million times as "the best thing I ever did in my whole life," stood beside his bed, running her fingers through his opulent head of hair, still as plush as a cotton thick mop. Although now sixty years old, with grown children of her own, Karen never tired of hearing her dad refer to her as his *sweet buttercup.* Her two older brothers, Tom Jr. and Jim, always knew she occupied a special place in their father's heart they could never rival. And it was fine with them.

Like a ping-pong ball lodged in the webbing of a catcher's mitt, her other hand rested in the palm of his. With hands like sculpted granite, Tom could crush a walnut in one while gently caressing a newborn in the other.

As tears welled in her eyes, Karen stared into the face of her father, at the plowed furrows etched deep into his cheeks and brow. She recalled the many times of her youth when her dad was her ultimate protector. How she hated him at times when he didn't approve of some *hard leg* (as he so elegantly put it), who stopped by the house to see her, only to leave and never return. Her husband Hal, a local banker in their hometown of Newnan, Georgia, stood behind his wife gently holding her shoulders as he too remembered his early encounters with his father-in-law. Particularly the day he came to see him at his store, with something specific he wanted to discuss. Hal had stopped by hundreds of times before, only this time he requested a private session with Tom in the back.

"May I have a few minutes with you in your office?" he asked, obviously nervous, voice crackling.

Tom tried not to smile, well aware of what this young boy had in mind. He had been dating his daughter for over a year and knew of the high regard in which his wife, and more importantly his daughter, held him. "I love him so much, daddy," she told him dozens of times. Truth be known, Tom held him in high regard as well.

"I don't expect you to be a perfect husband," he told him after Hal pronounced his intentions. "And I certainly don't expect there won't be tough times. Marriage isn't always easy. The rough patches, y'all will have to figure out on your own how to get through them. What I do expect is for you to always respect my daughter. And no matter how bad things might get, don't ever raise a hand to her. Not that I think you ever would, mind you, but it's something I need to say. It's the only line I'll draw. I'll come after you for something like that, and trust me when I tell you, people I come looking for don't want me to find them."

While stoic on the outside, Hal couldn't help but smile on the inside. It was pretty much exactly what Karen predicted her father would say. It's also what he wanted to hear. He had more respect for his future father-in-law than any person alive, perhaps the only exception being his own father.

The large contingent of family and friends, crowded together inside the tiny hospital room, all knew the end was near. Two of his three children and their spouses, along with six of his eight grandchildren and three of his four great-grandchildren, all held vigil beside his bed, waiting for the inevitable passing of the man they all knew as *Pop*.

"He doesn't seem to be in any pain," Tom Jr. said to Pop's cardiologist, who had stopped in to check on his patient and answer any questions his family members might have.

"Oh no, absolutely not," the doctor replied. "He's resting quite comfortably. All of his vitals look good right now. We're breathing for him to lessen the strain on his body, but we have the ventilator set extremely low. He could probably breathe on his own, but I don't really see the need for the added exertion. We'll take it out if he shows some signs of regaining strength and begins waking up. Right now, the most important thing is for your father to get as much rest as possible."

"I know we don't have much longer, doctor, but do you think we will be able to talk to him?" Tom Jr. asked.

"I think it's a real possibility," came the reply. "But probably not for several hours."

The duty nurse entered the room as the cardiologist concluded his conversation with Tom Jr. and the others present.

"Okay guys," she said upon entering. "Visiting hours ended a little while ago so I'm going to need everyone to go back to the waiting room so we can tend to him. Y'all can come back in a couple hours or so. I think some people from your church brought by some food. Smells pretty good. Go have a nice lunch and we'll come get you if anything in here changes. Your dad is doing great, especially for someone his age."

"You don't know the half of it," Tom Jr. replied as loved ones began to stand and exit the room, all delaying their departure to hear what the soon-to-be patriarch of the family had to say. "It's not just a miracle my dad made it to ninety-three. It's a miracle he was even born."

All of the family members knew Tom Jr. was referring to his Grandma Emma. It was a story told and retold over the years hundreds of times. Curious, Pop's doctor and nurse leaned in and listened as Tom Jr. told them of the miracle of his father's birth, and why Tom Sr. should never have been born.

***

<u>Montgomery, Alabama, 1910</u>:

Emma Whitaker was born into a working-class family in the Deep South and was a precocious child by the age of seven. While many of her childhood friends were the grandchildren of former slave owners, Emma's grandparents were southern tenant farmers. Unable to afford slaves, or even afford to own land, they leased acreage from a nearby plantation owner and made their living growing crops. After harvesting the crops and selling them at market, they used a portion of the money to pay back the landlord for use of the land.

Emma's dad, Mark Whitaker, a young boy when the Civil War ended in 1865, always held slave owners in contempt, and preached to Emma her whole life the evils of slavery. Whether it was out of genuine disdain for the abhorrent practice of slavery, or a tinge of jealously because he came from a family unable to afford to buy slaves, Emma could never be sure… she chose to believe the former.

As a tenant farmer for most of his life, Emma's grandfather often picked cotton from a 40-acre plot of land leased from a wealthy plantation owner on the outskirts of Montgomery, Alabama. As a young child, Mark Whitaker often worked the fields with his father and occasionally played with the children of some of the slaves owned by his father's landlord. Although he died before seeing the birth of his only grandchild, Emma's grandfather instilled in his son Mark the importance of hard work and the inherent respect all deserved, regardless of skin color or social status. Emma was raised with the same importance of integrity and respect for all.

In the earliest part of the twentieth century, especially in the Deep South, educating young girls was not considered to be of high import. Like many of the other social norms of the day, Emma's dad disagreed and would have nothing of it. Although only seven years old, Emma was taught to read at home by the light of a coal oil lamp and often accompanied her father to his tool and die shop located three blocks from the Alabama capital building on Dexter Avenue in downtown Montgomery.

Although Mark Whitaker knew carrying on the family business may not be his daughter's chosen profession one day, he wanted to instill in her a sense of independence and purpose, not leaving her future to be determined by the whims of some man.

He taught her how to take care of herself from an early age as well, stressing the importance of self-reliance. She was not likely to be pushed around by any of her playmates either, especially by some of the boys her age who believed in the superiority of their gender. Many young boys thought that way back then…and still do. Some grow out of it…some do not.

Two particularly mischievous boys her age walked by her father's shop one day and noticed Emma inside, alone, behind the counter. Hoping to generate a reaction from Emma by swiping something and taking off, one of the boys grabbed a hammer from a display rack inside the door and took off running, looking back to see if Emma would follow. And follow she did.

Running the two boys down from behind, she lunged onto the back of the boy with the hammer and tackled him to the ground, pressing his face into the street while prying the hammer from his hand. Without saying a word, she got up from the ground and calmly walked back to the store. Somewhat stunned, the boy got up and dusted himself off, saying a private prayer of thanks she didn't use the hammer to smash in his skull.

One late June afternoon, temperatures inside the shop reached triple digits. Emma's dad gave her permission to go outside and play with one of her friends who happened to be walking by the front of their shop with her parents. Excited for the temporary reprieve from the suffocating heat indoors, Emma ran outside in pursuit of her friend, no doubt hoping for a lick or two from the ice cream cone her friend was holding.

As Emma's bare feet hit the bricks of Dexter Avenue, she looked left and noticed her friend and her parents crossing the street. Emma moved in their direction and hollered out to her friend who had not yet noticed Emma's pursuit. Unwittingly, Emma had positioned herself directly behind a horse tied to one of the many hitching posts erected along both sides of the street. When Emma shouted to her friend, the sudden shriek of a seven-year-old girl startled the horse, causing him to violently kick his right rear leg in the direction of the disconcerting noise. The hoof of the horse impacted Emma in the center of her chest, knocking her ten feet backwards and face down in the street.

Mark Whitaker, hearing the commotion outside his shop, ran outside and found his daughter lying motionless on the ground. After immediately discerning what happened, he quickly scooped up the seemingly lifeless body of his beloved daughter and ran with her in his arms to the Watkins Infirmary located on Forest Avenue, approximately six blocks away. She was rushed inside the operating room to be attended to by the medical staff. An hour and a half later, a grim-faced Dr. Watkins approached Mark and his wife Bonnie, who had been fetched by the parents of Emma's friend so she could be by the bedside of her daughter.

"I'm not going to lie to you, Mr. and Mrs. Whitaker," Dr. Watkins began. "Your daughter's condition is dire. She has suffered tremendous trauma in her chest, causing quite a bit of bleeding on the inside. I've gone in to try and repair the damage and it seems as if the bleeding has stopped. There is still a great chance of infection developing around her heart, which could prove extremely problematic. We have her sedated, so she is in no pain. Right now, the only thing we can do is wait."

"Thank you, doctor," Emma's father replied, as her mother buried her face in her husband's chest, crying at the prospect of losing their only child.

Several minutes later, a woman approached Emma's mom and dad as they sat anxiously awaiting word about their daughter.

"Mr. and Mrs. Whitaker," the woman said as she sat beside them in the waiting room. "My name is Becky Neely. I'm from the Catoma Street Church of Christ and I do volunteer work here at the hospital. One of the nurses informed me of the condition of your daughter, and with your permission, I would like to visit her in her room and pray for her."

Although not a particularly religious man, Mark Whitaker was in no position to object. He and Bonnie were in a state of total despair and not likely to turn down any efforts by someone wanting to help.

"Of course, Miss Neely. If you think it will help," came Bonnie Whitaker's reply.

"Well, of course there are no guarantees Mrs. Whitaker," she responded with obvious care and concern. "But I truly believe in the Almighty's ability to heal. I would love for both of you to join me."

Moments later, the three of them were standing beside Emma's bed, tears flowing from each, as Miss Neely prayed earnestly for the Lord Jesus Christ to reach His healing hand down and heal young Emma, beseeching God for His favor in sparing the life of a most worthy child. The prayer session lasted less than ten minutes, with Miss Neely returning to the waiting room with Emma's parents to provide whatever additional comfort she could.

"Thank you for stopping by Miss Neely," Bonnie Whitaker said, as Becky excused herself to check on other patients and give care to others in need of her (and more importantly the Lord's) support. "We are certainly in your debt."

"I am honored to be of assistance," she replied as she put her arms around Emma's parents before leaving. "If it's alright with you, I would like to stop in tomorrow as well. As a matter of fact, I would like to stop by every day until your daughter is back to her old self again," she added with a smile.

Wiping the tears from his cheeks, Emma's dad smiled and nodded at Miss Neely as she departed the room.

True to her word, Becky came back the following day and the day after. Like clockwork, she showed up every day for eight days in a row. A ninth day's visit, however, would not be necessary. It was on this day Dr. Watkins burst into the waiting room to inform Emma's parents their daughter had awoken and was beginning to talk. Rushing to their daughter's hospital room, Mark and Bonnie Whitaker were consumed with unspeakable joy as they held Emma's hand and looked into her face, realizing they had their daughter back and she was going to be okay. Never again would Emma's dad doubt the sovereignty of an Almighty God. The experience would forever change him and would lead him and his wife Bonnie to accept the saving grace of their heavenly Father. It would similarly affect Emma and all those who came after her.

***

"Wow, what an amazing story," Pop's nurse quietly uttered, wiping a tear from her cheek as she smiled and looked down at her patient.

"So, you see doc," Tom Jr. continued, "without God's divine intervention in the life of my grandmother, none of us would be here right now. All of that happened fourteen years before my father was born."

"If you don't mind me asking, how long did your Grandma Emma live?" the nurse asked.

"She died while I was away at college," Tom Jr. replied. "She was seventy-one at the time."

"Well, she left quite a legacy," the cardiologist responded, as everyone left to reassemble in the waiting room, no doubt for the further regaling of stories about that very legacy.

CHAPTER TWO

Corn Pone and Hog Jowls

Sure enough, as Pop's nurse had previously reported, a large spread of home-cooked casseroles, buttery rolls, fried chicken and a plate of brownies awaited the Franks family when they returned to the waiting room. Delivered by a volunteer group from Newnan First United Methodist Church known as *The Ladies Service Group*, the meal was a welcomed respite from hours spent holding vigil beside Pop's bedside.

Tom Sr. (or Pop) and his wife Jackie joined Newnan First in 1975, shortly after moving to Newnan, Georgia. Daughter Karen, who wanted to become a pediatrician and was the youngest of their three children, was a freshman at Emory University in Atlanta at the time of their move. Tom Jr., the oldest, a Georgia Tech graduate, worked for an engineering firm in Atlanta and lived in nearby Peachtree City. Jim, completing his law degree at Emory Law School, was their middle child. He had already lined up a position with an Atlanta firm, and planned on living in Brookhaven, a suburban community north of Atlanta.

Jackie could not bear the thought of living so far away from her three children and convinced her husband the move was necessary for her to maintain her sanity. Always happy to oblige her wishes whenever he could, Tom consented to the move and promptly made an offer to purchase a feed and fertilizer store in Newnan.

After settling on the purchase of their new home, Tom and Jackie went about the task of finding a new church home. Grandma Emma had instilled in them both the need and relevance for maintaining a good relationship with *The Man Upstairs,* as she so eloquently referred to the Creator. The pastor of Newnan First, like Pop a retired farmer, instantly ingratiated himself to Tom and Jackie.

As Karen helped herself to a plate of food, she thanked the ladies who brought it and invited them to stay and join them for dinner and a visit. One of the ladies had been a dear friend to Karen's mom, having worked with Jackie Franks on many of the charity endeavors which consumed the latter stages of her life.

"We'd love to," came the reply. "I was hoping you'd invite us to stay," she added with a grin.

One of the ladies tending to the Franks family in their time of need was much more than a long-time church friend of Tom and Jackie. Her father, now deceased, was a local farmer who was one of Pop's earliest and most committed customers to his feed and fertilizer store. In fact, it was her father who first invited Tom Sr. and his wife Jackie to church soon after their move to Newnan.

"Tommy, you know how much your dad meant to my father and how much our whole family loves him," she commented. "I'm not sure you even knew this, or not, but when my dad was dying, your father came by the house almost every day to check on him, most of the time with his pickup truck loaded with bags of feed for the hogs."

"Yeah, I did know that," Tom Jr. replied with a smile. "Dad thought the world of your father. He was probably the best friend he had in this world." "Not hardly, Tom," she responded with a broad smile. "I'm pretty sure Miss Jackie had that title sewn up."

Ava, Pop's youngest great-grandchild, was polishing off her second brownie as she listened to the conversation between her great uncle Tommy and the nice woman who had brought the delicious treat now smeared across her precious face.

"So, you've known my Pop for a long time?" she asked, her ignorance to some of the family lore due to her relatively young age of seven. "And your dad and he were best friends?"

"They sure were, sweetie," Karen interjected, gently grabbing her granddaughter's hand and pulling her down in the chair next to her as she wiped her face with a napkin. "Miss Melanie's dad was one of the first people Pop met when he and Granny Jackie first moved here. Her daddy was also Pop's best customer."

One of the other ladies who had come with Miss Melanie to attend to the Franks family was much younger and not nearly as familiar with their family history. She knew them, of course, and often doted on *Mr. Tom* at church, as well as *Miss Jackie* when she was alive.

"I don't know why, but I always assumed you were from around here, Tom," she remarked. "I didn't know your mom and dad moved here from somewhere else. Where did you grow up?"

"My brother and sister and I were all born in Valdosta," Tom Jr. replied. "We grew up on our farm in a little town called Morven, a few miles from Valdosta. Mom and dad moved up here in 1975, after Karen graduated from high school and started at Emory. Jimmy and I were already living up here and I think my mom realized she was done with being a farmer's wife and wanted to live near her kids. Believe me, she usually got her way when it came to dealing with Pop. He used to tell me he wished he'd done it ten years earlier. They really loved it here, and all of y'all at their church were a big part of that."

"Why Newnan? How'd they end up here?" she asked.

"My mom grew up in Luverne, Alabama, a little town near Troy where my dad went to school," Tom Jr. answered. After she and my dad got married, they took a train over to Atlanta for their honeymoon. My mom really fell in love with the big city. She'd never seen buildings so big before. She told my dad at least once a month for the next twenty years how much she hoped to live there one day. They never got quite all the way to Atlanta, though, settling here in Newnan. Dad's best farming days were behind him and I think he wanted to try something new. Since farming was the only thing he had ever done in his life, buying his store kept him connected, I think, and seemed like a good idea. Anyhow, it got my mom within a few miles of all her kids, which seemed to please her. After all, I think pleasing my mom came to be Pop's main function in life."

"Where did Pop live when he was my age, Memaw?" Ava asked Karen.

"He grew up in the same place I did, sweetheart, in Morven, about two hundred miles south of here. Not too far from where I was born," replied Karen.

"What was Pop like when he was little like me?" Ava asked in the sweetest of tones.

A hush fell over the room, as everyone knew the question from young Ava became the perfect introduction to another story about Pop.

***

<u>Brooks County, Georgia, 1930:</u>

"Tommy, wash up and come inside, supper's ready," Emma Franks hollered out the front door to her youngest of four boys.

"Okay mom," six-year old Tommy Franks replied. "Watch this", he added, tossing a small tree branch across the yard, so proud to show his mom he taught his dog Amos how to fetch.

"That's great, honey, now wash up. Supper is getting cold," she replied.

Barely able to reach the metal pump handle above his head, Tommy pumped some water into the wooden bucket on the ground beside the well situated in their front yard, splashed water on his face and hands, and then went inside to eat. Amos assumed his usual position of reclining on the front porch, anticipating his own dinner would be forthcoming.

Emma Franks (nee Whitaker), now a young mother, lived in a five-room A-frame wooden home off Coffee Road in the small town of Morven, Georgia. Much to the chagrin of her mom and dad, Emma moved there nine years earlier after marrying Eddie Franks, the dashing young soldier she met at her father's tool and die shop in Montgomery.

Eight years her senior, Eddie had been born and raised in Wetumpka, Alabama, a cotton boom town located on the banks of the Coosa River, a little north of Montgomery. After several years of loading large crates of cotton onto steamboats headed for the

15

cotton markets of Mobile, Alabama, Eddie decided his life needed a major change in direction and vocation.

One particularly hot Alabama afternoon, as sweat poured profusely from Eddie's brow, a buddy of his ran up to him on the dock and told him he had signed up for duty in the United States Army and would soon be heading over to France to fight "a bunch of German idiots trying to take over the world."

"They're paying thirty-six dollars a month, all the free food you can eat and a carton of cigarettes a month," he proudly declared.

Dang, thought Eddie, *I need to get in on this deal.*

And so, he did. Boarding a train one month later bound for Camp Greene in Charlotte, North Carolina, Eddie wondered what he had gotten himself into. He'd never rode on a train before, or even wandered outside the boundaries of Elmore County, Alabama. After a few months of basic training, the newly minted *doughboy* found himself on an American steamship making its way across the Atlantic Ocean, bound for France.

As a member of the American Expeditionary Forces under the leadership of General John "Black Jack" Pershing, Eddie took little time in experiencing his first bit of real fighting in *The War to End All Wars*. Manning a Vickers .303 British machine gun, Marine Private Franks helped American and French forces stave off a German assault near the Marne River, a mere fifty miles from Paris, as part of Germany's *Spring Offensive*.

After German commanders ordered an advance on American and French positions along the river, the U.S. Marine commander, General James Harbord, countermanded an order from his French superior to retreat further back, instead ordering his men to dig trenches where they were and hold their position. After digging shallow fighting trenches in the dirt with their bayonets, from which they could fight from the prone position, Private Franks and the rest of his unit waited on the imminent German assault. When the enemy got within a hundred yards, the U.S. Marines opened fire, mowing down waves of German soldiers and forcing them to retreat into the nearby woods.

Known as The *Battle of Belleau Wood,* the fight Eddie and his fellow soldiers had engaged in was far from over at this point. After forming a defensive line along the Paris-Metz Highway, German forces dug in and reinforced their position with additional troops. After the U.S. Marines were repeatedly urged to turn back by retreating French forces, Eddie's Marine captain responded, "Retreat, Hell. We just got here." After two more days of intense fighting, the German assault finally had been repelled.

Although the U.S. involvement in World War I did not officially end until 1921, the *Treaty of Versailles* signed with Germany in 1919 effectively ended Eddie Franks' time in harm's way. Discharged from service later in the year, Private Franks returned to Alabama…a local hero of sorts.

In the spring of 1920, Thomas Kilby, Alabama's 36th governor, organized a parade in the state's capital city to honor those Alabamians who heroically served their country in *The Great War.* Standing outside the front door of her father's shop on Dexter Avenue, Emma Whitaker saw Eddie Franks for the first time and was immediately smitten. Handsome and debonair in his military dress, the sun gleaming off his polished shoes like a reflection in a mirror, Eddie couldn't help but notice the beautiful young lady watching him as the procession of Alabama heroes passed by.

When the procession reached the Whitaker Tool and Die storefront, on their way to the steps of the state capital building, hundreds of people lining both sides of the street began waving American flags and throwing confetti over the heads of their heroes. Eddie, however, noticed neither the confetti nor anyone else in the cheering throng. His eyes were locked on the pretty, young seventeen-year-old smiling and waving at him as he passed. When the festivities concluded an hour later, he made a beeline back to where he first saw her standing outside her father's store.

"Hi, I'm Eddie," he said, extending his hand to her, as she stood behind the counter of the shop, only a few feet from the watchful eye of her father. Correctly assuming the skeptical look coming from the man beside her belonged to her dad, Eddie quickly turned his attention to him. Reaching out his hand, Eddie introduced himself to Emma's father. "Eddie Franks, sir, it's a pleasure to meet you."

"The pleasure is mine," Mark Whitaker replied. "Thank you for your service to our country. Are you from around here?"

"Yes sir, I am," Eddie replied. "Wetumpka, actually. A little north of here."

"I know it well," Emma's dad responded, not oblivious to the nature of Eddie's visit, and quite aware of the infatuation apparent in his daughter's face. "May I introduce you to my daughter, Emma Whitaker."

"It's a real pleasure to meet you, Emma," Eddie said, returning his attention in her direction.

After an uncomfortable pause in dialogue, Mr. Whitaker attempted to fill the void in the conversation.

"May I invite you to our home for supper?" he asked Eddie. "Emma's mom is a very good cook and we would be honored for you to join us."

"Yes sir, Mr. Whitaker," Eddie replied with little hesitation. "I'd love to."

"Emma, why don't you escort Eddie home and let your mother know he will be joining us for supper," her father said. "I can close up here and be along shortly."

For the next four months, the two young lovebirds spent virtually every waking hour in each other's company. Completely mesmerized by stories of his time spent in France and other European countries (minus the grizzly details of what it's like to be in battle while killing men who are trying to kill you), Emma was fast falling head over heels in love with Eddie. And the feeling was mutual.

Six months later they were married in the chapel of the Catoma Street Church of Christ, home church of the Whitaker family since experiencing a divine intervention in their daughter's hospital room years earlier. Following their nuptials, the newlyweds moved into a small two-room cottage located in the back yard of Emma's home, a tool shed converted into living quarters by her dad, no doubt wanting to keep his only child close.

The move from Montgomery, Alabama, to Morven, Georgia, would take place the following year. After Eddie's grandfather passed away, he left a 200-acre tobacco farm to Eddie. Reluctant as she had been to move away from the only home she had ever known, as well as her parents whom she dearly loved, Emma knew her place now would be with her husband. It was also the chance to start their life together on their own, outside the shadow of her parents, and continue growing their family, which had already grown by one, with their second child already on the way. Although sad about the upcoming separation they knew to be imminent, Mark and Bonnie Whitaker knew the move provided their daughter and son-in-law more and better opportunities than they would ever have if they stayed.

"Oh, it's really not so far," Emma's dad assured his wife, with only a modicum of success. "No more than half a day's drive."

Eddie poured himself into learning the tobacco farming trade, while Emma concentrated on having babies and providing their family a comfortable home.

Emma had been raised in Montgomery, Alabama, the state's capital city and one-time capital of the Confederacy. Jefferson Davis took the oath of office as the duly elected President of the Confederate States of America, two football fields away from where her daddy would later open his shop for business. She was a city girl through and through, born and reared in a city where the majority of streets were paved with bricks. Although her own parents were never able to afford it, Emma loved visiting one of her childhood friends who lived nearby, whose parents owned a home with indoor plumbing.

"You can't hardly believe it momma," she remarked to her mother, after coming home from a visit with her friend and seeing their bathroom. "You can go pee or take a bath and never have to leave the house! I've never seen anything quite like it."

***

Morven, Georgia, was quite a different kettle of fish. The nearest brick-paved street was fifteen miles away in the city of Valdosta, at one time the richest city in America based on per capita income, a level of wealth due almost entirely to the booming cotton trade. When the Atlantic and Gulf Railroad Company decided to run its tracks all the way to Valdosta in the 1860s, the city gained access to the rest of the country, ever hungry for King Cotton. Eddie Franks' grandfather, who willed his land to Eddie upon his death, had grown cotton on his land for more than sixty years and made a pretty good living doing it. But something happened about ten years before he died, which made growing cotton at a profit nearly impossible.

A tiny beetle, not much bigger than a man's thumb, somehow migrated into the U.S. from Mexico, and then proceeded to make its way clear across the South, infesting every cotton field in existence along the way. The Boll Weevil, as it was known, effectively destroyed the cotton industry in the Southern U.S. states, taking most of the jobs and wealth associated with the industry with it. Like most cotton farmers at the time, Eddie's grandfather had to make a decision about what now to grow on his land, believing cotton no longer had much of a future.

Corn, beans, potatoes and the like were an option he considered, but the competition in these crops would be immense, thus making his potential return on investment less attractive.

Tobacco, he rightfully surmised, was where the future of his land needed to go. Europe had been a huge market for tobacco products, and America was on its way to becoming one. Snuff and loose-leaf tobacco for pipe smoking were already very popular, but the invention of a cigarette rolling machine in the late 1880s made cigarettes cheaper and more accessible to the masses. Tobacco,

Eddie's grandfather figured, could be even more profitable than cotton. He was not wrong.

Eddie, unfortunately, inherited his grandfather's land but not his cultivating skills. The first year he tried growing his crop of tobacco, he failed to properly guard against something known as *Blue Mold,* which effectively wiped out most of his plants. The first couple of years, in fact, were replete with failures and lost crops, making it difficult for Eddie to keep his head above water. What little profit existed, hardly ever made it to Emma's hands.

Those first few years, Emma occasionally splurged on herself by buying a new pair of shoes and a dress…perhaps once a year at most. Occasionally, she took her boys into town and treated them to a chocolate malt or maybe some peppermint sticks at the local drug store.

This was the life Eddie Franks had delivered Emma into. She tended a vegetable garden beside their house, growing corn, tomatoes, green beans, field peas and turnips. All of which served as supplements to the bacon, pork chops and other hog products she received from their neighbor, whom they affectionately knew as *Old Man Jenkins*.

Mr. Jenkins ran a pig farm on his property and gave the meat to Emma in exchange for her tutoring his five grandchildren who lived with him. A wood-burning stove Eddie purchased from Montgomery Ward as a wedding gift for Emma was the only household item they brought when they made the move from Alabama. A metal stovepipe run from the back of the stove to an exhaust vent mounted on the wall of the kitchen provided Eddie and his boys a daily reminder of when supper would be served.

Black billowing smoke could be seen from anywhere on their property, indicating supper preparation was underway. When the smoke stopped, it was time to come inside and eat. James, the eldest of the four Franks boys, kept his momma's wood box full of firewood as his daily chore. Almost ten years old, he was the only one of the children their momma could trust with an axe.

Emma Franks had become quite proficient at preparing and cooking the Southern cuisine her family enjoyed. She kept them well fed with menu items known to *stick to the ribs* of healthy, growing boys.

"I'm so hungry, I could eat the south end of a north-bound mule!" Eddie often said, causing his boys to burst with laughter every time he said it.

"There you go again, Eddie, teaching the boys something they ought not need to hear," came Emma's usual reply.

Three cast iron skillets were Emma's most indispensable items in her kitchen. Corn pone, a derivation of cornbread but made without milk or eggs, filled one of the skillets on a daily basis. Ham hocks or hog jowls could often be found stewing in another, with loads of turnip greens mixed in. Little Tommy especially loved crumbling up his corn pone and soaking it in the juices of the stew before consumption. Occasionally, Eddie would bring home some nice cuts of beef steak, usually gotten from the local butcher through some sort of barter. Fresh vegetables would always round out their meal, with plenty of leftovers for the following day's lunch.

On special occasions, or when she felt her boys deserved a treat (which was often), Emma would chop up the meat from a few sugarcane stalks and melt it on top of the stove. After being left to cool, the boys would take turns breaking off chunks of the sweet, hardened candy resting in the bottom of the skillet. It wasn't a horrible life by any stretch. They never wanted for food, or much of anything. But it could have been better...and it took a while before it was.

CHAPTER THREE

Treein' 'Coons

Young Tommy and his three older brothers, James, Earl and Bobby, loved to place pennies on the railroad tracks, which ran by about a mile east of their property, and wait for a train to come by and flatten them.

"You're wasting perfectly good money, boys. Not a one of you have the good sense God gave a goose," their mother told them often.

The boys didn't see it their mom's way, however. It was money they earned and it's exactly how they wanted to *spend* it. James, Earl, Bobby and Tommy were entrepreneurs, of sorts, in their own right, making pretty good money for boys so young. Tommy's dog, Amos, was a key factor in their success.

Amos was a Catahoula Leopard Dog, given to Tommy as a Christmas gift from their neighbor with the pig farm, Old Man Jenkins. When the early settlers of America first moved into what is now Louisiana, they discovered the woods were overrun with wild hogs. Subsequently, the Catahoula had been bred as a *hog dog*, trained to drive hogs and other livestock to slaughter. Weighing nearly eighty-five pounds, Amos outweighed his master by a good twenty pounds.

"Look at his eyes, momma, they're different colors," he remarked upon meeting Amos for the first time.

"Yes," Emma replied, immediately falling in love with him, too. "He sure is a handsome dog."

Emma asked each of her boys to chip in with ideas for a name. After considering *Buddy, Bentley* and *Rebel* (Emma's choice), Tommy settled on *Amos*.

"It's in the Bible, momma," he concluded.

A loyal friend and protector, especially to Tommy who slept beside him every night, Amos had a menacing bark and vicious presence, especially to anyone who might approach their house unannounced. He usually tended to his guard duty from his position on the front porch and would never allow anyone to get close to the front door unless accompanied by a member of his family. If Amos knew you were all right, then he would wag his tail and attempt to lick you to death. If not, he would try to eat you alive, or at least make you think he would.

A couple of days a week Emma would make a big batch of cathead biscuits in one of her iron skillets. Right after removing them from the oven, while still smoldering hot, she would pour a ladle full of melted butter over the tops of the biscuits. Before the butter had time to soak in all the way, she would sprinkle a spoon-full of sugar across the top, making sure a sufficient amount stuck to the hot, wet butter. It happened to be her boys' favorite treat. After placing the succulent, mouth-watering treats on the windowsill leading out to the front porch to cool, Emma would holler to her boys playing in the yard to come and get one. She seldom had to call them twice.

One afternoon, Bobby happened to be a tad late getting to the front porch to claim his share of the four biscuits set out by their mother. As James, Earl and Tommy began devouring their treat, Bobby hit the steps of the front porch in full stride and reached the edge of the windowsill at the same moment as did Amos. Amos had decided the fourth biscuit, unclaimed at this point, became fair game for anyone to consume, particularly himself. As his mouth made contact with the biscuit, removing it from its perch on the sill, Amos was set upon from behind by Bobby; adamant their dog was not going to enjoy their momma's treat meant for him.

Bobby's hands went straight to Amos' mouth as both of their bodies crashed on the wooden planks of the front porch. Trying to wedge one of his hands inside his mouth to prevent Amos from swallowing the biscuit, he used his other hand to squeeze his nose and poke him in his eyes, all the while attempting to bite him on the back of his neck. He determined to get his biscuit back and was relentless in accomplishing this task.

With a dogged determination never before seen by his three brothers, Bobby finally pried open Amos' jaws and retrieved his sought-after biscuit. Standing up after the wrestling match concluded, with Bobby the clear victor, he walked off the front porch, biscuit firmly secured in his hand, and made his way towards the water well in the front yard. Tommy followed his brother down the steps, all the while looking at the biscuit in his brother's hand, now a mangled mass of dough, dripping with Amos' saliva.

"Whatcha gonna do with that biscuit Bobby?" he asked, a bit stunned at what he had just seen.

Reaching up to the top of the well pump handle, far out of Amos' reach, Bobby carefully placed the biscuit down, making sure all the wet portions faced directly into the sun.

"It just needs to dry out a little, Tommy," he replied. "Once it does, it'll be just fine to eat."

***

Several months after Amos had become a member of the family, James ran into the house one afternoon and breathlessly stated, "there's an old woman in town paying fifty cents for a dead raccoon."

"Fifty cents?" Earl exclaimed in utter disbelief. "For one raccoon? Tar nation, James, we got a woods full o' em."

The woman James referred to was known by everyone in town as *Miss Lissy,* an elderly black woman who spent most of her life in the employ of rich white families, raising their babies and performing household tasks like washing and ironing their clothes. She stumbled upon her new profession one day when a lady for whom she worked came home wearing a new fur coat, made from raccoon pelts.

"How much do sumpin' like that cost?" she asked.

"Almost ninety dollars," her employer replied.

"Lawd have mercy, ma'am," Lissy replied. With a big smile and a laugh, she added, "You white people is plum crazy."

It also gave Miss Lissy an idea for a new venture of her own.

She set up shop under an old tent at the corner of Gordon and Park streets, near the train depot and right next to a large peach stand, where peaches had been sold for decades. Besides local consumers, she figured she could market to some of the people passing through on the rail line.

After skinning the 'coon, she would clean the pelt and let it dry in the sun. A cast iron kettle with a raging fire underneath, used to cook the meat, rested beside Miss Lissy under the shade of her tent. Considered by many a Southerner as a *delicacy,* her raccoon meat was seasoned with the perfect amount of Cajun spices and salt. Seldom, if ever, were there any leftovers at the end of the day. "Taste just like chicken," she told her customers.

The main staple of her new business had been 'coonskin caps and neck warmers. Additionally, many of the young boys in Morven liked to run around town with a raccoon tail hanging from a belt loop or pocket, the easiest thing for her to make. The real money was to be made in full-sized fur blankets or coats, provided she had enough skins to do the job. If the Franks boys had their way, she would soon be sitting on a surplus of pelts.

Raccoons are nocturnal animals, spending most of their daylight hours asleep, usually inside a hollowed-out tree or a rotten log. Though they will eat almost anything, their preferred diet consists of sweet berries, fruits and insects. Their evenings are spent almost exclusively foraging for food.

Amos began his training as a *'coon dog* after James discovered a raccoon corpse laying in the middle of Coffee Road, near their house, killed by a passing car or truck the previous evening. The three boys, excited to get started on their new venture (no doubt with visions of dollar signs in their heads), tied the dead raccoon to the end of a stick with a piece of their mother's kitchen apron. For the next several days they dragged the stinking carcass around the yard in front of Amos, constantly rewarding him with treats of bacon for recognizing its scent.

"Get that smelly thing out of this house!" Emma shouted to James, the one and only time he brought the *training* stick inside and attempted to leave it on the fireplace hearth.

"Use your head for something besides a hat rack, son!" Eddie chimed in. A phrase he often used whenever one of his boys did something he deemed idiotic. This certainly fit into such a category.

"Can we go out tonight after supper, daddy?" Earl asked, as he and his brothers cleared the supper dishes from the table, depositing them in Emma's wash bin beside the stove. "We want to start getting some 'coons."

Eddie looked at Emma with a slight smile on his lips as James, Bobby and Tommy froze in place awaiting an answer from their dad to Earl's question.

"I don't see why not," Eddie replied. "If y'all think Amos is ready."

"Oh, he's ready, daddy," Tommy interjected. "He's the smartest dog I ever saw."

As soon as it got dark, Eddie headed out with his four boys in tow, a flashlight in one hand and a .22 rifle in the other. Tommy had not yet become big and strong enough to hold Amos back on his leash, should he pick up the scent of a raccoon, so the job fell to James. As they entered a patch of woods a mere twenty yards behind their house, Amos tensed up, rigid as a board, at the first scent of his prey.

"Release him James," his father commanded. "Let's see him go to work."

As soon as he untied the rope, tied with a granny knot around his collar, Amos took off like a flash in pursuit of his first conquest.

"C'mon boys, let's follow him!" Eddie shouted to his sons, unable to hide his own excitement.

In a matter of moments, the hunters had caught up to Amos, his hind legs planted firmly on the ground with his front legs resting up the trunk of a sweetgum tree. Barking vociferously at the raccoon perched on a branch, fifteen feet above his snarling snout, Amos kept guard over his prey, giving his masters time to move in for capture.

"He's treed one, daddy!" Tommy shouted, his voice full of excitement, his chest about to burst open with pride.

"Shine the light up there. I think I see 'em," James added, he too in a temporary state of euphoria.

Earl, now holding the flashlight, moved the light beam up the trunk of the tree until it reached the bright, shining eyes of their prey.

"Hold still everybody," Eddie said to his boys, as he slowly unslung the rifle hanging over his shoulder.

"Hold the light real steady," he instructed Earl, as he brought the rifle to eye level and pressed the stock into his shoulder. "Go ahead and tie him up, James," he added. "We don't want Amos to chew him up once he hits the ground."

After Amos had been adequately restrained and pulled back away from the tree, Eddie fired one shot at the raccoon, hitting him squarely between its eyes, causing him to fall from its perch and land with a thud on the ground below.

"You got 'em, dad," Tommy shouted, as he pulled an empty cotton flour sack from beneath his shirt, one of four he had brought along to carry home what he hoped would be a banner haul of raccoon carcasses.

They got seven the first night, nine the next, and eight more the next.

"Do you think we'll run out of 'em?" Tommy asked his big brother James following their third night of hunting, seemingly concerned about the limited supply of prey.

"No way, Tommy," James assured his little brother. "There's more out here than we'll ever be able to get. We'll wear out Amos long before we run outta 'coons, I can tell you that right now."

Sighing with relief, Tommy reached over and put his arms around Amos, resting comfortably on the front porch after another successful night of hunting.

"Good boy, Amos, good boy," Tommy whispered to his best friend, rubbing the top of his head while Earl, James and Bobby sat counting their three-night haul.

"We better get these to Miss Lissy pretty soon," James remarked. "They won't be worth squat if we let 'em rot."

The three younger brothers all nodded in assent, confident in their older brother's sage assessment.

'Coon hunting with Amos would become a regular activity for the Franks boys over the next several years. After a couple of months of hunting with their dad, James was deemed by their father old enough, and responsible enough, to handle rifle duties, allowing them to go out at night on their own. Earl, Bobby and Tommy would eventually assume rifle duty as well, all becoming quite efficient in the use of a gun. Efficiency the four brothers would need later in life.

CHAPTER FOUR

Throwin' A Conniption

Newnan, Georgia, established in 1828, is the county seat of Coweta County, Georgia. Situated a few miles south of Atlanta, many of its early settlers were doctors, lawyers and merchants, a significantly more professional class of people than many of the rural towns it neighbored.

When Union General William Tecumseh Sherman conducted his infamous *March to the Sea,* burning everything in sight from Atlanta to Savannah after informing his superiors he wanted to "make Georgia howl," Newnan had been left relatively untouched. This was primarily due to the fact Newnan had been a hospital town throughout the war, where many Confederate soldiers were treated and convalesced after being wounded. Apparently, *Uncle Billy* had a temporary case of sympathy for the invalid.

Although not nearly as populated or as cosmopolitan as its big sister to the north, Newnan nonetheless takes a backseat to no one when it comes to providing medical care and services to its citizens. Piedmont Newnan Hospital, a state-of-the-art medical facility with top-notch doctors and medical personnel, is the current and likely final home of Tom Franks, Sr.

Residents of present-day Newnan enjoy many of the same perks available to those living in much larger cities around the country. Ashley Park, a sprawling shopping complex with major retail chains and upscale restaurants, opened for business a few short years ago. Soccer fields and baseball diamonds litter the landscape of Newnan and surrounding Coweta County, providing an ample number of venues to grow their burgeoning youth sports programs, vital to building the character of its youngest citizens. Children of all ages, from many different ethnic backgrounds, can be found playing sports together twelve months out of the year, a sight unfamiliar to Pop as a child growing up in South Georgia.

Tom Jr., along with his wife Rachel, left the hospital and returned home to nearby Peachtree City, in much need of some rest after spending the last twelve hours at his father's bedside.

"Go home and get some rest, Tom," his sister Karen told him, "let some of us take the night shift. You've been here all day. If anything with dad changes, we'll call you right away."

"Thanks Karen, I think I'll take you up on that," he replied. "Lord knows I can use some rest."

An hour later he sat in his recliner watching Fox News on T.V., catching up on the latest news. As he listened to some talking head drone on about current race relations in the United States, he couldn't help but think about his dad lying in a hospital room and how far the country had come since his dad had been a boy.

"The Bible tells us God created everyone equal," Pop told his three children at least a thousand times over the years. "And He meant everybody. Black, white, green or purple, don't matter the color. We're all the same in His eyes."

Sentiments he no doubt got from his sainted mother. Unfortunately, as a young boy growing up in the South, many of those around Tom and the rest of his family failed to share those same sentiments.

***

<u>Valdosta, Georgia, 1935:</u>

Although a relatively small city in terms of its population compared to Atlanta, some two hundred and thirty miles to the north, Valdosta had been a major hub for commerce due to the rail service emanating from its downtown area.

By 1935, much of the cotton industry had returned to pre-Boll Weevil levels once farmers figured out how to kill the pesky little bugs. Cotton prices, which had dipped substantially during the first few years of the *Depression*, were on their way back to normalcy. In addition to cotton, soybean and tobacco crops were enjoying a surge in worldwide popularity, as many South Georgia farmers began rotating their crops each year between the three.

Soybean, an inexpensive source of both oil and protein, was not only suitable for human consumption, but had been used in feed for livestock and other animals. Cigarette and cigar sales in the U.S. were booming, providing the farmers of tobacco crops a relatively comfortable source of income.

Valdosta and its surrounding communities were flush with money, at least compared to many other cities and towns in the U.S., still trying to recover from the *Depression*. Eddie Franks had come a long way in figuring out how best to grow tobacco, and he too began taking part in the economic surge.

Although the scourge of slavery had been vanquished nearly seventy years earlier, many descendants of those slaves were under the employ of white landowners, hired to pick the crops of several southern farms. Some of the white employers, never quite resigned

36

to the fact the South lost the Civil War, were none too equitable in the treatment of their hired hands.

One such employer was a man named Cyrus Hampton, who owned four hundred acres of prime farmland outside the city limits of Valdosta. Passed along to him from his father and grandfather, the farmland had once been a plantation worked by slaves owned by Mr. Hampton's ancestors. A six thousand square-foot antebellum home, built by slaves nearly a hundred years earlier, still proudly stood on the property.

Jonathan Sydney was a black farmhand who had been in Mr. Hampton's employ for over ten years. He and his family, along with the families of six other farmhands, lived in a bunkhouse on the property. Mr. Hampton, not known as a particularly gracious employer, had always treated his employees as if slavery still existed on his farm.

One day, Jonathan's wife and twelve-year-old daughter were at work inside Mr. Hampton's home, performing typical household chores, when Mr. Hampton approached the daughter. He became visibly upset when he observed the manner in which she was cleaning the silver.

"You worthless little *nigger*," he shouted at her, causing her to immediately burst into tears. For some inexplicable reason, he then slapped the young girl across her face.

The girl's mother, who witnessed the entire episode, ran to her daughter's defense, and was likewise slapped across the face by Mr. Hampton.

"Get the hell outta my house," he yelled, causing both to run out of the house in tears, back to their bunkhouse. When Jonathan saw his wife and daughter so visibly upset and crying uncontrollably, he asked his wife to tell him what happened. After hearing his wife's version of the abuse visited upon her and their daughter by Mr. Hampton, Jonathan retrieved a pistol from his room and set out to confront his employer. In spite of his wife's pleading for him not to go, Jonathan was not about to let the incident go unchecked.

When he reached the front porch of the house, Mr. Hampton confronted him, telling him if he knew what was good for him, he'd turn "his black ass around" and head back home. Jonathan Sydney could not control his rage. He pulled the gun out from underneath his shirt and proceeded to shoot Cyrus Hampton four times in the chest. Mr. Hampton was dead before his body hit the ground.

Jonathan ran back to the bunkhouse and gathered his wife and daughter and fled the property, hiding out at his cousin's house in town. When another farmhand found Mr. Hampton's dead body lying on the front porch of his home, he ran into town and informed the sheriff. Within the hour, a large lynch mob began to form outside the sheriff's office, filled with enraged men intent on seeking justice for the wanton killing of a most revered citizen in their town by a black man.

The mob set out in seek of revenge, ransacking houses all over Brooks County, looking for the black scoundrel who had committed the unpardonable sin of shooting and killing a white man. Eventually, the crowd of men, thirsty for blood, found Jonathan and his family hiding under the porch of his cousin's dilapidated wooden house about five miles from the scene of the crime.

The mob descended upon Jonathan, his wife and daughter, and the other three people inside the house…Jonathan's cousin and his two teenage sons. All six were summarily lynched by the vicious mob, hanged from the branches of two large white oaks growing in the front yard of the home. They had their revenge, unmoved by their act of sheer barbarism.

The sheriff, who happened to be a deacon in one of the local churches, stood behind the crowd and refused to participate in the murders of at least five completely innocent people. Yet, he did nothing to prevent the barbaric act.

James, Earl, Bobby and Tommy Franks, concluding a recent transaction of raccoon pelts with Miss Lissy, saw much of the commotion underway when the lynch mob made their rounds through town. Intrigued by the activities afoot, they ran after the mob and followed them to the home where Jonathan Sydney and his family were ultimately found. Hiding behind a row of Georgia pines adjacent to the property, the boys' presence had not been noticed by the sheriff or anyone else in the mob, as they witnessed the atrocities committed by the murderous mob.

Scared and upset, they stayed hidden in the woods for several hours before returning home. By the time they walked in the front door of their house, word of the event had reached the ears of Emma and Eddie; oblivious to the fact their sons had witnessed the entire thing.

Most upset by the incident was Tommy, who couldn't stop crying as he and his brothers relayed to their parents exactly what they had seen.

"It's pure evil," Emma said to her boys. "We'll get through this as a family, but I hope you never forget what you saw (as if any chance existed the boys could ever shake the memory of such a horrendous act). The Lord judges us all, and those evil men will one day receive theirs. Don't you boys ever forget that."

"We won't momma," James replied on behalf of his brothers.

And they never would.

At the ripe age of eleven, Tommy Franks had witnessed something no young boy should ever have to see. He and his brothers had been exposed to a level of hatred unfathomable between fellow human beings. They knew about slavery and how many of the white people in the South could not get over the fact it had been abolished, the result of a war where close to half a million Americans died in order for it to end.

Eddie and Emma had taught their boys all about *The War Between the States* and why such a dreadful thing occurred. They also taught them how important it is to show respect to all people, regardless of the color of their skin. Tommy, for one, could never understand the sentiment prevalent in the hearts of so many of their neighbors. Miss Lissy, a black woman, was someone he revered, a woman he considered one of his best friends, despite their obvious difference in age, background and color. And she had come to love the Franks boys as well, most especially Tommy, who always gave her a hug after concluding their business.

Unfortunately, more displays of the rampant hatred and divisions associated with racial bigotry in the South would rear its ugly head, and little Tommy would not escape having to see a lot of it. Years later, he would bear witness to examples of human depravity on such a grand scale, as to forever alter his belief in what some men are capable of.

***

In 1865, when Confederate General Robert E. Lee walked into the Appomattox Courthouse outside Lynchburg, Virginia, to meet with Union General U.S. Grant, he did so with the intent of signing an order of surrender, essentially ending the bloodiest period in American history.

Following the end of the *Civil War*, the United States quickly moved into what is known as the *Era of Reconstruction,* designed to heal a broken nation by reconciling with Southern states who had sought independence, and providing Constitutional freedom to the slaves emancipated as a result of the defeat suffered by the Confederacy. Many in the South, however, were unwilling to sign on to the notion of reconciliation, believing in the superiority of the White race and intent on denying black Americans their God-given rights.

This sentiment, unfortunately, led to the creation of the *Ku Klux Klan* by a few former Confederate soldiers from Tennessee. Their ugly hatred and bigotry had been on full display for a nation to see, trying to heal from the ravages of a bloody war. After a few short years, with the bodies of hundreds of murdered black Americans and the charred remnants of burned down schools and churches in their wake, the *Klan* was effectively put out of business by the collective efforts of *decent* people, unwilling to tolerate such abhorrent behavior.

By the time of the Valdosta lynching in 1935, for which Tommy and his brothers bore witness, the *Ku Klux Klan* had been undergoing a bit of a renaissance. Following the murders perpetrated upon Jonathan Sydney and members of his family, the *Klan* in South Georgia began holding meetings out in the open, no longer feeling the need to keep their activities hidden from view.

Contributing to this newfound boldness had been the obvious bigotry towards Blacks and Jews, which seemed to emanate from the offices of politically elected officials and other *upstanding* citizens of the community. So many police chiefs, sheriffs and their deputies, deacons and pastors attended *Klan* rallies, cloaked in white robes and masks decrying the assault on *the good white people* of America by those less worthy.

Klan members and sympathizers spent a lot of time in recruitment efforts in and around Brooks County. Having been approached on multiple occasions to join their movement, Eddie Franks would have none of it. The third time a *Klansman* visited Eddie at his home, trying to get him to sign up and *help the cause*, Eddie asked the man to accompany him to his toolshed behind their house to talk further. The man obliged, thinking Eddie only wanted to speak in private, away from his wife and children.

Once inside the toolshed, Eddie latched the door shut and reached for a sickle hanging on the inside wall. Gently pushing the man backwards against the door, Eddie held the 30-inch razor-sharp steel blade against the man's throat and looked him square in the eyes, now protruding from their sockets.

"The next time one of you gutless weasels trespass on my land, asking me to join your pathetic group" he said, with no ambiguity in his voice, "I'm going to take this here sickle and slit you in two! Have I made myself entirely clear?"

The man's feet barely touched the ground as he made haste across Eddie's front yard, leaving a rooster tail of dirt and rocks behind the tires of his pickup truck as he screeched away. Eddie left no doubt in the man's mind where he stood on the issue. A fourth attempt to recruit Eddie Franks to *the cause* would not be forthcoming.

No retribution targeted at Eddie for denying their advances would come either; primarily because he had always been regarded as a local war hero, having bravely fought in the *Great War.* It may well also have been because of whom Eddie was married to. Emma Franks had a reputation of being someone not to wrangle with. A reputation she had earned with distinction.

***

A couple of years earlier Emma had stopped by the dress shop in town, seeing if there might be something new she needed. The shop's clerk was a friend from church and felt bold enough to tell Emma about something bothering her regarding her husband Eddie.

The clerk had noticed how much attention Eddie seemed to receive from one of the waitresses at the local diner…particularly when he stopped in without Emma. The waitress was a young woman, much younger than Eddie, whose husband had run off with another woman several years earlier. Emma's friend had become alarmed at what she felt were inappropriate advances being made towards Eddie by the waitress, and felt Emma should be made aware.

Concerned by this new revelation, Emma took care to come into town several times over the next few weeks and *peek* in at the diner when she knew Eddie would be there. Sure enough, as her friend had informed her, the waitress went out of her way to pay special attention to Eddie, completely oblivious to the overtures being made his way. He probably thought the young waitress was simply being nice, not realizing she had targeted him to be a worthy recipient of her affections.

Emma, on the contrary, had no such misperception of the intent of the young, attractive waitress. The following day, without saying anything to her husband, she visited the diner to confront the waitress, knowing Eddie would be home at work in his fields.

Walking into the crowded restaurant, filled with patrons enjoying plates of chicken-fried steak and fried okra, Emma approached the waitress now standing behind a long lunch counter, pouring sweet iced tea into a customer's glass. The look on Emma's face was hard to miss, and even harder to misunderstand.

The waitress froze in place as Emma approached, her steely eyes boring a hole through the waitress. Without saying a single word, Emma reached across the counter and grabbed the waitress by the back of her hair, pulling her over the top of the lunch counter. As dishes and silverware (not to mention a full pitcher of sweet tea) crashed and broke on the floor of the diner, Emma dragged the poor woman kicking and screaming all the way across the floor and out the front door.

Once outside, Emma proceeded to slap, kick and punch the young woman senseless, all under the watchful eyes of a diner full of people, in utter shock of what they were witnessing. Only after Emma believed she had gotten her message across did the whipping cease.

The message had been loudly and clearly received, and no such infractions by the young woman ever occurred again. The townspeople got a message as well: Emma Franks was not someone to be trifled with.

In due time, Eddie learned of the events involving his wife, and like most men, had the capacity to be dumber than a bag of hammers. In this instance, however, he exhibited the wisdom of a savant. He never once mentioned the incident to his wife.

CHAPTER FIVE

Gettin' Your 'Shine On

It took Eddie a few years, but he eventually began to show an ability to grow and cultivate tobacco crops with a certain degree of efficiency, and by the summer of 1935 began showing a decent profit. All of his boys were heavily involved in the venture, working the fields with their dad and participating in the family business. During the school year, the boys would get up early in the morning and put in a couple of hours before school, and then usually work until dark after getting home.

Late February or early March signaled the beginning of the tobacco-growing season in South Georgia. After tilling up the ground in preparation for planting, Eddie used long planks of pine boards, made from trees he and his boys cut down on their land, to form the planting beds for the seeds needed to grow his tobacco plants.

After spreading the seeds throughout the various beds, the boys would gently rake the seeds into the ground, making sure all were covered with dirt. Once this step had been accomplished, nails were driven around the edges of the wooded frames, with a thin layer of cheesecloth attached to the nails and pulled taut over the top of the beds.

The cloth protected the seeds from the cold and wind, allowing them the opportunity to germinate and grow into strong, healthy plants. On days when the sun was bright, the boys would roll the cloth away and let the sunlight penetrate the ground and help the seeds grow. Once the weather warmed and the seeds began to turn into plants, the cloth would be entirely removed.

After the planting beds produced an allotment of viable tobacco plants, it became time for Eddie and his boys to move the plants out to the field, transplanting them in rows of cultivated ground not used for tobacco the previous year. Rotating the crops every year into dirt where corn or beans were grown the previous year would help his tobacco plants avoid getting infected with various diseases. This had been an expensive lesson Eddie learned the hard way, losing multiple crops to disease in previous years.

Settin' out day, when the plants were moved from the beds to the field, usually took place in early April and was an exciting day for the Franks family. The success of the entire planting year would depend on it. After filling up on scrambled eggs, bacon and grits, with a side of biscuits and gravy, the long workday would commence.

After pulling the plants from their beds and carefully placing them in cardboard boxes for transport to the field, ever mindful not to damage the roots, Tommy would walk behind his dad or one of his brothers, busy punching holes in the dirt where the plants would go. After dropping the plants into their holes, Tommy reached down with his hands, making sure to scoop and press enough dirt around the base of the plants to secure them into the ground. Tommy took great pride in his task, forming an almost emotional relationship with each plant. Emma came behind Tommy with a wooden bucket filled with water and gave each plant a drink before moving on to the next.

The succulent stems and leaves of a tobacco plant provide food for several types of bugs, insects and worms, and had become something Eddie had to contend with as soon as the plants were in the ground. Tommy and his brothers went out once a day, checking each plant for predators and picking off the Cutworms, which seemed to move in overnight.

After punching several holes in the bottom of a cardboard box, Eddie would fill the box with powdered insecticide, which his boys would then use to *dust* the plants, killing off the bugs too small or plentiful to remove by hand. Instead of coming home from school and playing in the yard, or shooting squirrels in the woods, the boys had to man a hoe and remove the weeds growing around their tobacco plants. All of this work became necessary if Eddie and his family were to enjoy the profits of their tobacco crop several months hence.

Like typical boys their ages, the Franks brothers were not always happy in their roles of *indentured servitude.* Sometimes, this led to ill moods and testy dispositions between them, ultimately leading to physical confrontations. As most brothers fight from time to time, the Franks boys were no exception.

Being the youngest and smallest, Tommy had to deal with being pushed around by his older brothers, made to do the menial tasks they were intent on avoiding. Not yet big enough to fight back, he had to put up with it in those early years. James, being the oldest, assumed the position of *leader* and often bossed his younger brothers around when their mom and dad were absent.

He had to rethink his position of authority one day after an encounter with his brother Earl. Although a year younger than James, Earl was nearly the same size as his older brother and had begun showing signs of what his mother deemed to be "hot-headedness."

After concluding a workday out in the fields, the four brothers sat in the back of their dad's pickup truck as he drove them all back to the house for supper. After driving through the gate leading out to their field, Eddie stopped the truck so one of his boys could hop out and close the gate before continuing on to the house.

"Get out and shut the gate," James said to Earl, motioning him with his hand to jump off the back and accomplish the task.

"You do it, James," Earl retorted. "I shut it yesterday."

Not pleased with the challenge to his authority, James reached forward with both hands and shoved Earl in the chest, causing him to fall out of the back of the truck.

"I said shut the gate!" he repeated, as Earl stood up and dusted off the back of his pants.

Earl turned around and walked over to the open gate, pulled it closed and brought the latch down, securing the gate to the fencepost. He then hopped back in the back of the truck without saying a word, as their dad pulled away and headed for home, having observed the scene in his rearview mirror. Tommy and Bobby looked at James, who had a smile on his face; confident in the fact his authority had been reestablished.

When the four boys got out of the truck and began walking towards the house, Earl hung back, seemingly dejected about being manhandled by his older brother. Unbeknownst to his brothers, Earl had grabbed a four-foot-long piece of timber from the bed of the truck before jumping out. Wielding it like a baseball bat, he approached James from behind and swung it as hard as he could at his older brother, catching him square between his shoulder blades as he reached the bottom step to the porch. The blow knocked James forward, causing him to crash-land into a rocking chair, bruising his hands and knees in the process.

In stunned disbelief, Tommy, Bobby and Eddie could only stop and stare as Earl dropped the board on the ground and walked past the groaning body of his older brother, prostrate on the porch, trying to figure out what had hit him.

Earl opened the front door and walked inside without saying a word.

Eddie, ever mindful of the reason for the ambush, said nothing and followed his sons inside. *It's between the brothers,* he thought. *They'll work it out.* As he walked through the front door, the palm of his hand covered his mouth, so the slight smirk on his face could not be seen.

***

Tending to his crop all the way through growing season needed Eddie's daily attention. It was a process he had learned, and every step in the process became vital to being a successful grower. As his tobacco plants matured, blooms began to form, which required their removal in order to enhance the growth of the tobacco leaves, which is where the profit comes from. Snapping off the blooms by hand is known as *topping off* the plants.

After accomplishing this part of the process, additional buds, or *suckers*, would begin to form on the plant stalks, denying necessary nutrients to the leaves. Removing these *suckers* (known as *suckering the plant*) also had to be done by hand and had always been the most hated of all tobacco farming jobs. The boys would come inside after a day of *suckering,* covered head to toe in sticky, tobacco tar.

In late June or early July, after the tobacco leaves had reached complete maturity, it became time for the Franks boys to harvest their crop. *Puttin'-in* the tobacco was the most exciting time of the year for Tommy and his brothers, as it signaled the end of the growing season and all the hard work associated with it. After pulling off all the tobacco leaves by hand, the boys loaded the leaves into the back of a wagon and hauled them into the tobacco barn. Once inside the barn, Eddie and Emma tied the leaves to long *tobacco sticks*, which were hung from the rafters inside the barn so the leaves could *cure*. A furnace, kept lit on the floor of the barn round-the-clock, provided the heat necessary for proper *curing.*

After concluding the *curing* process, which usually lasted five or six days, the *cured* leaves would be loaded into the back of Eddie's truck and taken to the auction barn in Hahira to be sold, hopefully at a nice profit. This part of the *process* became a time of pure joy for the Franks boys. Seeing how hard work and dedication to a task can result in a successful conclusion was a character-building exercise Tommy and his brothers never forgot. It also was the type of character-building Tommy would eventually pass along to his children and grandchildren.

***

The Withlacoochee River forms part of the boundary line between Brooks and Lowndes County, Georgia. Brownish in tint from the Georgia red clay washed into it from the rain, it runs south into Florida, eventually dumping itself into the Gulf of America. Most days, when Tommy and his brothers were not either in school or working their daddy's fields, they could be found hanging out along the banks of the river, skipping rocks, fishing for catfish, or splashing around to cool their bodies from the intense heat of a South Georgia summer.

When the river flooded from torrential downpours of rain, the water level reached some of the lower hanging branches of trees along the banks. As the water receded, some of the dirt on the banks would be washed away. Over the last century, this process had caused the creation of large crevasses along the banks of the river, over which hung the twisted, exposed roots of some of the trees, longing to sip the water from the river below and trying their best to stay rooted in the disappearing ground. Snapping turtles as big as the hubcap from a large truck, with jaws strong enough to snap the wood handle of a garden hoe in two, could often be found floating in these crevasses. Tommy was scared to death of these turtles.

"Turtles ain't nothin' Tommy. It's the gators you gotta be afraid of," his brother Earl told him, providing Tommy not a scintilla of comfort.

The thick woods on both sides of the river were popular for local moonshiners to cook their brew…with ready access to the river for a quick escape should the *Revenuers* move in to shut them down and make arrests. On many occasions during their youth, Tommy and his brothers happened upon an abandoned still, usually left in pieces by a *Revenue Man* who found it and chopped it up with an axe, denying its owners the privilege of ever using it again. The boys always wondered if the owners of the still got away, or were currently locked up somewhere, paying their debt to society for their misdeeds.

***

Making moonshine, especially in the South, had become a booming business after the federal government passed *The Prohibition Act of 1920.* People all around Brooks, Cook and Lowndes counties made tons of money running moonshine throughout the South when Tommy had been a young lad, much of this newfound wealth frivolously squandered away.

When *Prohibition* was repealed in 1933, only a moderate decline in the production of moonshine in South Georgia could be seen. Old habits are hard to die sometimes. Although alcohol could now be bought and sold legally, the legal stuff rarely matched the intensity and effect of an expertly made jug of *White Lightning.*

Hanging outside of *Granny's Sundries* in downtown Morven, a local store where townspeople could buy anything from a can of snuff to a box of soap, often provided the Franks boys with well-needed entertainment. Some of the old men in town, whose wives had either run off or were dead, sat around on turned over water buckets spinning tales and bragging about something they had done or seen.

They wore the same thing every day, probably because it was all they had. Liberty overall jumpers, with Long Johns underneath in the winter, and hobnail boots made up their wardrobe. With callused hands and skin as coarse as cracked leather, their faces belied their true age. Most looked decades older than they actually were, brought on by years spent in the hot sun, plowing fields or hauling lumber. The *smart* ones, which were few and far between, had gotten past the third or fourth grade and were able to read. It had been a hard life for the men of this time, and it was a life Eddie and Emma were intent on their boys avoiding.

A large jug of moonshine was always a part of these sessions, passed from man to man until the last drop had been consumed. Although the conversation often veered off into areas not suitable for younger audiences, it was not likely this group of men had the capacity to practice discretion.

If the adage is true, which says God looks after children and fools, then it made sense why some of these old drunks were still above ground. One day, while James and Earl went inside the sundry store to pick up a box of lye soap for their momma, Tommy and Bobby remained outside listening to the men talk, as their conversation appeared to take an ugly turn.

Joe Lee Warren, known by everyone in town as *Pud*, was already three sheets to the wind, with his jug of 'shine still half full. He apparently took offense at a comment made by one of his drinking buddies known as *Scooter*. After *Pud* had gone on about how *sorry* his ex-wife was for running out on him with some *ass wipe* from Valdosta, *Scooter*, clumsily attempting to agree with his friend, commented about her looks, saying she was "not particularly fond looking as well."

Clearly a violation of an unwritten rule about Southern men disparaging the woman of another, regardless of whether or not the woman was his ex, *Pud's* pride got hold of him and he felt the need to respond accordingly.

"Ah hell, *Scooter*, like you got room to talk," *Pud* retorted. "Your damn wife, God rest her soul, looked like she fell out of an ugly tree and hit every branch on the way down. And you know that's no damn lie, neither," he finished, reaching down for another long swig from his jug.

And with that, the battle began. *Scooter*, equally inebriated and quite wobbly when he tried to stand, got up and charged *Pud* who had just insulted his former wife, now deceased. He either jumped on top of *Pud* or fell into him…Tommy and Bobby could never be sure…wildly swinging his fists as *Pud* did his best to set his jug on the ground without spilling any of its content.

As *Pud* screamed, "Get your fat ass off me, *Scooter*!" he inadvertently shoved his hand inside *Scooter's* mouth, pushing on his face in defense of the assault mounted against him. *Scooter*, in a state of drunken rage, promptly bit down on one of *Pud's* fingers and began shaking his head back and forth like a dog chewing on a ham bone.

Two other men, party to the initial confab and witnesses to the entire incident, made no effort to move in and halt the altercation, opting instead to reach for *Pud's* jug, saving it from any damage it might sustain in the melee. About two minutes after it had begun, the fight ended, primarily because neither man was in shape enough to jog around the block, much less fight another full-grown man.

Pud pulled an old grease rag out of the pocket of his overalls and wrapped it around his finger, while wiping the stream of blood down his arm on his pants leg. *Scooter*, after rolling over from atop his friend, used all the strength he could muster just to get to his feet.

"Dad-gummit, Scooter. You nearly bit my cotton-pickin' finger off!" *Pud* remarked, reaching down with his good hand to set his water bucket back in place so he could sit down again. "Gimme back the jug" he added, looking in the direction of the man who had saved his 'shine from certain destruction.

"Well, I swanee, *Pud*," *Scooter* replied, "You got me madder than a wet hen. You shouldn't never a said sumpin' so mean about my wife. Even if it is true," he added with a smile.

"I reckon you're right, I guess," *Pud* replied, turning his jug up and taking a long slug. "She was a pretty good ol' broad from what I remember."

And so, it ended as quickly as it had begun. The two men not participating in the battle laughed at *Pud*, who continued shaking his hand, slinging droplets of blood in the dirt. The pain would come later, when the moonshine coursing through his veins had time to dissipate…perhaps a day or two away.

Tommy gave James and Earl a blow-by-blow description of the fight as the four boys walked home, he and Bobby laughing about it the whole way.

CHAPTER SIX

Sittin' Up with the Dead

Tommy and Amos had been virtually inseparable since the moment Old Man Jenkins brought the speckled puppy by the Franks home, five Christmases past. Big and strong now, Amos weighed close to ninety pounds. His master and best friend, thanks to the biscuits and gravy, hog jowls and fat back used to cook most meals, had surpassed Amos in both girth and weight.

They ran everywhere they went. Through the woods, up and down Coffee Road, or any other dirt road they travelled, always seeming to be in a hurry. They weren't, of course, it's just the way they preferred to travel. Emma, not wanting to appear to be in a contest with her son for Amos' affection, tried not to let on how much she loved the little guy as well. But love him she did.

Amos loved Tommy and was fiercely loyal to him, but he had no misunderstandings about who "buttered his bread," never passing on a chance to slink up beside Emma if she happened to be anywhere near her kitchen stove. Emma was not shy about *accidentally* dropping a hunk of corn pone or a pork chop bone on the ground in front of Amos, never looking at him, of course, since feeding Amos directly from the supper table had been forbidden in their home.

Walking through the front door one evening after a visit to town, Eddie had sad news to share with his family. His elderly Aunt Helen, who grew up in Eddie and Emma's home as a young girl, only to move a few miles away after marrying, passed away after having been in declining health for some time.

She and her husband, who had preceded her in death by more than twenty years, were long-time members of the Mt. Zion United Methodist Church in Morven. Known simply as *Campground* by all the locals, the church had been founded and built a century earlier by her husband's ancestors. Eddie and Emma attended *Campground* on a regular basis, having baptized all four of their children there.

At a time when funeral homes were few and far between…the closest one being in downtown Valdosta…it became a common practice for a deceased body to lay in repose overnight, either in their home or inside the church where the funeral service would be held the following day.

Several weeks before her ultimate demise, Aunt Helen asked Eddie to make her a coffin from a tall poplar tree out behind his house, a tree she had climbed hundreds of times as a little girl. He was more than happy to oblige her.

After lining the inside of the coffin with cotton batting, Eddie covered the batting with a soft crepe fabric, ensuring maximum comfort for his aunt when the Lord finally called her home. Before laying Aunt Helen in her final resting place, some ladies from Mr. Zion came by the church to fix her hair and don her in her favorite pink chiffon dress. Bright red lipstick and a touch of rouge completed the preparation for Aunt Helen's trip to Glory, where she would meet her Maker face to face.

Part of the grieving process for Southern departed souls often included loud hollering and screaming, a practice exclusively reserved for only the closest living blood relatives. It was heavily frowned upon, and considered quite unseemly, when such a tradition was violated. Whispers of "she's only a second cousin," and the like, would easily spread through the crowd like wildfire if someone contravened this well-established tenet.

Another tradition involving the passing of a loved one in the South was known as *sittin' up with the dead*. Some say the tradition began as a way to keep rodents and other creepy, crawly creatures away from the body on their final night above ground. Most people simply believed it was the proper thing to do, not letting one's loved one spend their final night alone.

On the afternoon prior to Aunt Helen's burial the following morning, her body had been transported to the church and laid to rest in the coffin Eddie had built. Friends and family from all over Brooks County stopped by the church, many carrying plates of fried chicken, boiled ham, deviled eggs, baskets of supper rolls, and fresh fruits and garden vegetables. They all wanted Aunt Helen to go out in style, celebrating her life with a plethora of good, down-home Southern cookin'.

Tommy and Bobby, who had not yet participated in the time-honored tradition of *sittin' up with the dead,* were told by their father it would be their responsibility to sit up with Aunt Helen, making sure she would have the company of loved ones as she spent her last night on God's earth. James and Earl, who had previously sat up with one of Old Man Jenkins' farmhands several months before, immediately slid over to the corner of the church, whispering to one another and conspiring about playing a trick on their two younger brothers.

As day turned to night, Aunt Helen's loved ones and friends began leaving the church to head back home, carrying with them their empty plates and what little bit of leftovers had not been eaten. Emma made sure to leave behind some fried chicken and buttermilk biscuits for her boys, in case they got hungry during the night. James and Earl told their folks they'd be home shortly, right after stopping by the river to check on some of their catfish traps. It was a ruse, of course, as the boys wanted to hang back and hopefully torment their little brothers.

With everyone gone and the coast clear, James snuck up to the front of the church and gently knocked on the door, while Earl ducked down out of sight beneath a window in the back. Tommy and Bobby, having taken their positions for the night on one of the pews a few feet from Aunt Helen, spun their heads around at the sound of the knock.

"Someone's knockin' on the door," Bobby said to Tommy, "stay here and I'll go see who it is."

"No way Bobby, you're not leaving me here alone," Tommy replied, too scared to even think about being this close to Aunt Helen alone. "I'll go with you."

Both boys made their way to the door, slowly opened it, and peeked through the crack to see their brother James on the other side.

"James, what are you doing here?" Bobby asked with a huge sigh of relief in his voice.

"Mom wanted me to make sure you guys saw the fried chicken she left," he replied. "She was worried y'all might get hungry tonight."

"Yeah, we saw it," Tommy replied, "I've already had two pieces. You wanna stay with us, James?" he added, hoping for the additional protection he knew his older brother would provide.

"Nah, I better get on home," James said. "Y'all have fun tonight and I'll see ya in the mornin'. And make sure you watch out for ghosts, they been known to come out at night around here," he concluded, a big smile forming on his face as he turned to walk away.

The diversion at the front door had given Earl the opportunity to climb through the window without Tommy or Bobby seeing him. Once inside, he tiptoed over to where Aunt Helen lay and slipped underneath the bed sheet covering the table holding her casket. After the door closed in front of him, James ran around to the back of the church and ducked down out of sight below the window Earl had climbed through. He wanted to be sure he was present to hear his little brothers' reaction to the plan he and Earl had hatched for them.

After laying perfectly still and quiet for several minutes, listening to Tommy and Bobby talk about various things, Earl waited for a lull in their conversation. Eerily silent inside the church, the only sounds to be heard were the cicadas singing outside the window and the slight rustle of tree leaves being blown by the night breeze. As low as he could, Earl softly moaned for two or three seconds and then went silent.

Tommy and Bobby immediately sat up erect, placed their hands on the back of the pew in front of them, and looked at each other with wide eyes and open mouths.

"Did you hear that?" Tommy asked in a whisper.

"Yeah," Bobby replied, also whispering. "I heard it. What do you think it was?"

"I don't know, Bobby, but I don't like it," Tommy said, making no effort to hide his sudden concern.

From his position of cover underneath Aunt Helen, Earl placed a hand over his mouth so not to let out a laugh. He waited a few minutes and began to moan again, only this time a little louder.

Tommy and Bobby were still frozen in the same position when the moaning resumed. As fast as two boys could move, Tommy and Bobby jumped to their feet and ran out of the church, both believing Aunt Helen had somehow been brought back to life. They ran all the way home and burst through their front door, completely out of breath and barely able to speak.

"Mom, it's Aunt Helen," Bobby said to his mother, startled by their sudden entry. "I think she's come back to life."

With a look of astonishment, Emma looked at Bobby, then at Tommy, and back to Bobby.

"What do you mean she came back to life?" she asked incredulously. "Have you boys lost your ever-lovin' minds?"

At about this time, James and Earl came in the house, also out of breath from running as fast as they could to catch up to their brothers. Both were laughing hysterically, slapping each other on the backs and rolling around on the floor. Emma knew immediately they had been up to something and were no doubt responsible for Tommy and Bobby's state of panic.

After taking several minutes to calm down, James and Earl were able to speak and told their mother what they had done. Somehow, Emma kept from smiling, instead feigning anger at her two oldest sons.

"All right, you two smarty-britches," she said, looking James and Earl in the eyes. "Looks like y'all will be going back up there to sit with Aunt Helen. And not only that, but you'll be doing all the chores around here for the next week. Now get on outta here, both of ya."

Walking back to Mt. Zion church, James and Earl could not stop laughing. Although they both felt their punishment a bit harsh, in the end, they concluded it was worth it.

CHAPTER SEVEN

Done Been Kilt

Except for James, who was born in his granddaddy's tool shed behind the house in Montgomery, Emma gave birth to her boys in the front room of their home in Morven, on an old hand-me-down cotton mattress Eddie had traded a couple of chickens for. The midwife, who brought the boys into the world, looked like she could've been at least a hundred years old, and very well may have been. Hardly bigger than a well-used bar of soap, you could've added a foot to her height just by ironing out her wrinkles.

Nobody in town could remember a time when the old woman wasn't around, and birthin' babies was the only thing anyone had ever seen her do. Since there wasn't a lot of money back then, she got paid whatever the new parents could afford. Some half-worn clothing, a chicken, maybe a cut-up hog; she got whatever she could talk them out of. She even provided her services for as little as a batch of cathead biscuits.

Emma finished having her babies before her twenty-third birthday. James, not old enough to remember when Earl and Bobby were born, always remembered the day Tommy entered this life. The sound of his momma screaming as Tommy made his entry into the world scared James to death, but he wouldn't let on. Somehow, his little mind figured she had enough to worry about without being concerned with him.

After the pain stopped and he could see the tears of joy on his momma's face, James knew everything would be all right. He sat quietly beside his new little brother as the midwife dunked a rag in a bowl of warm water and wiped him down, not unlike his father polishing the fender of his Ford pickup. Looking at his little brother for the first time, James never knew a human being could be so small.

I'm going to take care of you, he quietly thought. And he pretty much did.

There were plenty of times growing up when the brothers beat on each other. It's just what brothers did. And James had no qualms about setting any of his younger brothers straight when he thought they were getting out of line. But don't make the mistake of messing with them if you were outside the family. Many a time James beat the living snot out of some other kid in town who made the mistake of raising a hand to one of his brothers…Tommy especially. Tommy always looked at James as his protector, and he rarely failed in the task.

When the *Depression* hit, it caused a lot of pain throughout the country, and South Georgia was not immune. Cotton prices plummeted, which affected many of the growers in the South. Eddie didn't even know what a stock market was, so the crash in 1929 had no effect on him, at least not directly. The Franks could still grow vegetables and get eggs from their chickens, while Emma continued to help educate Old Man Jenkins' grandchildren for some well-appreciated cuts of pork. Despite the problems rampant everywhere, people still needed tobacco to smoke in their pipes and cigarettes, and enjoy an occasional can of snuff, making Eddie's plight less severe than most. But not everyone in and around Brooks County was as fortunate as the Franks.

***

Cockfighting had been a popular sport in the South for as long as anyone could remember. During the *Great Depression,* a lot of men around town used the sport to supplement their meager incomes. Of course, where there's a winner there must also be a loser, and sometimes a man losing the last dollar to his name led to states of desperation and despair. Occasionally, a man would lose his life over a match deemed rigged, or one in which the loser was just plain unlucky. Tommy witnessed one such occasion inside the barn of one their neighbors.

Emma didn't much like her boys going to watch cockfights, but sometimes boys don't always do what their mommas tell them. Locked from the inside to keep out the unwanted, namely the sheriff and his deputies, the neighbor's barn teemed with activity as a round of cockfights were underway. Tommy slipped inside through an opening in the wall left by a busted-out wood plank, probably the result of being kicked out by an angry mule.

Dozens of men surrounded a make-shift arena, tossing coins and dollar bills on the ground inside the cockpit, wagering on which combatant would ultimately prevail in the death match. One guy, obviously short of legal tender, was allowed to place his bet in the form of a five-pound block of government cheese, no doubt intended to be food for his family.

Tommy, mesmerized by all the hollering and arguing taking place as matches were won and lost, saw grown men close to tears as small fortunes were wiped away, while others showed exuberance over their well-earned victories. One of the men who lost, despondent over the prospect of going home empty-handed, accused the man he lost to of being "an out-and-out cheat," a charge not looked upon lightly by these men.

"What do you mean I cheated?" the offended man and victor in the match replied. "You better take it back, you sumbitch, or you're gonna end up face down in this here pit like your pathetic bird."

The man making the accusation, who had no facts to support such a specious charge, reached into the bib of his overalls and retrieved a pocketknife, which he began waving around in the air above his head. It got relatively quiet as men backed away, anticipating a different kind of death match, but were nonetheless eager to witness.

The man with the knife jumped over the chicken wire surrounding the cockpit and lunged at the man who had just won the last dollar to his name. The unarmed man under attack could do little to defend himself, as his attacker's knife plunged deep into his gut. Tommy could only stare in disbelief as he watched the aggrieved man continue stabbing his victim, over and over again until the man's overalls were soaked with blood.

"Damn, I think he's kilt," remarked one astonished viewer.

"You're gonna fry for this, you son-of-a-gun," yelled another, as the man fled the barn, crashing clear through the barn door on his way out.

Tommy had seen a dead man before, like the time he and his brothers saw those poor people lynched a while back. Only then, it had been from afar, while the boys were hidden behind a row of trees and bushes several yards away. This was up close and personal, and it was something a young boy should never have to see.

Tommy had always been a good son, who loved his mother more than anything. He confided in her and shared with her his innermost thoughts and fears, rarely ever holding anything back. This, however, was something he would take to his grave. Not even his brothers would find out he had been inside the barn this day, a witness to the murder of a man over losing twenty dollars on a bet.

Sure enough, the guilty man was caught a few hours later, hiding out at home in the loft of his hay barn. When the deputies came for him, he didn't put up much of a fight. He probably knew it would be pointless. About a year later, after being tried and convicted for murder, a couple of Georgia State Corrections officers strapped the man's arms and legs to *Old Sparky* (Georgia's electric chair, at the state prison in Reidsville) and sent a bolt of lightning through his body, frying him to death. It had been exactly what the man at the cockpit had predicted, when the guilty man ran out of the barn after committing his crime.

When Tommy made it back to his house after his surreptitious trip to the cockfight barn, a commotion of some sort had gotten underway at home. He joined his three brothers on the front porch, who were leaning in near the front door, trying to hear what their parents were discussing. Their mom, obviously upset about something, could be heard crying as she attempted to explain to Eddie what had upset her.

"What's wrong, James?" Tommy asked his brother.

"Hush, Tommy," came the reply. "Something happened over at Old Man Jenkins' place. Got momma real upset. She came home crying a little while ago. That's all we know right now."

A few minutes later Eddie came outside on the front porch where the boys stood, each with a look of concern on their face. Their concern seemed to escalate when they saw the shotgun in their father's hand.

"James, go get in the truck, we're takin' a trip," he told his oldest boy.

James did as his father told him, and the two of them rode off in a hurry. Where they were headed the other boys could only guess. Obviously concerned about the welfare of their mother, the boys ran inside to tend to her, who seemed to be calming down.

"Mom, what happened?" Earl asked, as Bobby and Tommy looked at their mother with concern.

Apparently, what upset Emma took place at the Jenkins place earlier in the afternoon during a tutoring session with his grandchildren. As Emma listened to the children read to her under the shade of a large White Oak in his front yard, a large, menacing hound dog belonging to one of the neighbors wandered into the yard, growling at the children as he approached. Obviously frightened, the children jumped up and ran around behind Emma seeking protection, as the mangy dog continued to bare its teeth at the children.

Emboldened by the fear he could sense coming from the children and Emma, the dog moved in closer as Emma shouted at the dog to leave them alone. The youngest child, a six-year-old girl, panicked and decided to make a run for it, leaving the protection of the group in an attempt to make it inside the house.

The dog bolted for the little girl and caught her from behind, sinking its teeth into the back of one of her legs. Emma rushed over to try and save her, kicking the dog and punching it in the back, while the other children screamed and cried. The owner of the dog, a man named Cletus, appeared through the woods across the yard and whistled for his dog to return. The dog released his clamp on the little girl's leg and ran off, but not before inflicting significant damage to her tiny leg.

Cletus, an ornery old codger who lived alone, had never been well liked by anyone in town. He didn't even have the decency to check on the girl before disappearing back into the woods with his mutt.

Emma picked up the little girl and rushed her inside the house where her wounds could receive proper attention. Her single mother cried hysterically as she and Emma wrapped bandages around the wound. Despite her own tears, Emma seethed with anger. Old Man Jenkins, she knew, was too old to go and confront Cletus over what happened. Her Eddie, however, would be far less inclined to let something like this go unchallenged after she explained to him what happened. On this count, she had been absolutely correct.

After hearing a loud knock on his door, one he was not surprised to hear, Cletus cracked open the door and saw Eddie and James standing on his front porch.

"What's the gun for, Eddie?" he asked, peering through the crack.

"I think you already know, Cletus," Eddie replied. "Now where's your dog, I come for him."

"Well, you can't have 'em," Cletus shot back. "You and your boy need to get off my porch and go back home."

"Then it that case, I come for you, Cletus," Eddie responded forcefully. "It's your choice. I'll only ask you one more time. Where is he?"

"He's in the barn," came the reply, as the door quickly shut.

James got back in the truck as his father instructed him to do and patiently sat as he watched his father open the door to the barn. Half a minute later he heard the sound of a shotgun blast reverberate inside the barn. Eddie got back in the truck, laid the shotgun in the gun rack behind the seat, and drove off without saying a word.

CHAPTER EIGHT

Do-Hickies and Creosote Poles

Dot Edwards is Pop's oldest living relative. Thirteen years his junior, she has known Tom Franks all her life. During the entirety of her eighty years on this earth, she has never lived more than five miles from her current home in Adel, Georgia, located about fifteen miles from the Franks tobacco farm in Morven. Never quite sure if she was his second cousin or first cousin once removed (the second description never made sense to Pop), Dot is known by everyone as simply *Miss Dot.* For the past thirty-five years she has been in charge of putting together a yearly family reunion, always held the first Saturday and Sunday in May at *Campground.*

Carloads of relatives come from miles around to sit in church, sing hymns, and listen to the preacher man deliver a sermon, usually wrought with messages of fire and brimstone and eternal damnation for those who die without being *saved.* Following the service, usually concluded with one verse of *Bringing in the Sheaves,* everyone is invited to go outside and enjoy a nice lunch provided by *The Ladies Auxiliary Group.*

Dozens of casserole dishes, buckets of fried chicken, and plates of cookies and cupcakes adorn a procession of folding tables lined up end-to-end outside the church. Nearly half a football field in length, the tables are covered with butcher paper, taped in place to keep from being blown away by the wind. A few cans of bug spray are available to help keep the large contingent of sand fleas and gnats from invading the population. Their assault on the plates of food, however, cannot be defended. In these parts, swallowing a few gnats along with your spoonful of corn chowder is simply tolerated. Pop's parents and his three brothers are buried in the old cemetery adjacent to the church, where several headstones bear the *Franks* name. When Pop's final days on earth have concluded, he too will find his final resting place here.

When Tom Jr. called Miss Dot to tell her of his father's condition, suggesting it had gotten close to the end, she asked one of her granddaughters to drive her to Newnan so she could see Pop one last time.

"I know I'll be seeing him in Glory soon enough," she told Tom Jr., who insisted there was no need for her to make the grueling trip north at her age. "But, by God, if I have to walk up there to see him before he leaves this earth, I'm a gonna do it."

Tom Jr. knew there was no need arguing with her.

"You come on then, Miss Dot," he replied. "Y'all can stay with Rachel and me. We'd love to have ya."

The drive north up Interstate 75 was void of much conversation between Miss Dot and her granddaughter. As Taylor Swift's latest CD quietly played over the car's sound system, Miss Dot sat in the passenger side of the front seat, looking at the countryside go by in her window, reflecting on her life and how much Pop had been a part of it.

***

<u>Morven, Georgia, 1941:</u>

After walking through the door from church, Emma got busy in her kitchen getting ready for company they were expecting later in the evening. Eddie's cousin from Adel was coming down for a visit and Emma wanted to have a banquet-style feast waiting on them when they arrived. Fresh corn, buttermilk biscuits, collards, ham hock stew and pork chops were on the menu. Their Adel kin loved coming to visit them on their farm, especially their daughter Dorothy, who would be celebrating her fourth birthday with them.

Dot, as everyone knew her, loved coming to the farm for a variety of reasons. She loved all her cousins, but especially Tommy, who would set her inside a cardboard box, punch a hole in the side where he could attach a rope, and then drag her all over the yard.

There was also Amos. Standing upright, Dot's face was nose-to-nose with Amos, and she never tired of him licking her to death, laughing incessantly the whole time. Amos, beginning to show his age a bit, had become a much less rambunctious dog, spending more time than ever reclined on the front porch. But like he had been when Tommy was small, Amos viewed himself as Dot's protector, like the time she wandered upon a rattlesnake sunbathing beneath a tobacco stalk the previous year. Somehow recognizing the danger, Amos nudged her back with his snout and positioned his body between her and it, barking viciously at the serpent until it slithered away.

A couple of years earlier, the Georgia Railway and Electric Company had begun sinking creosote light poles in the ground all over Brooks County, stringing wires across the top and bringing electricity to an area devoid of the modern-day convenience. Electricity had become commonplace in big cities like Valdosta and Atlanta, and now it had reached Eddie and Emma's farm. A Crosby Companion cathedral-style radio, housed in a beautifully finished red oak box, sat proudly on a small table beside the fireplace in the Franks' home. Never a fan of daily serials like *The Guiding Light* and *Painted Dreams*…known as *soap operas* because advertisers peddled soap to the audience made up almost entirely of housewives…Emma's favorite program was *Our Gal Sunday,* a show about a small-town girl who marries an English aristocrat.

"Nothin' but nonsense," Eddie told her about a thousand times.

The only show he liked to listen to was a crime drama called *Gang Busters.* The boys loved it as well.

As Emma and Dot's mother cleared away the supper dishes from the table after all had been sufficiently fed, Eddie turned on the radio, hoping he hadn't missed the opening of his favorite show. Instead of hearing the familiar voice of the man who opened the broadcast each week, Edward R. Murrow, a famous news reporter from New York, had been telling the nation about an attack by Japanese planes on Pearl Harbor, a U.S. military base in Hawaii. Everyone knew about the war raging over in Europe, and a man named *Hitler* causing so many problems. The attack by the Japanese, however, came as a total shock to most. Eddie, having spent time in war some years earlier, had a sinking feeling about what this would mean.

With looks of concern on the faces of everyone present, Eddie looked at Emma and said, "We're going to war, honey."

He wasn't wrong.

***

Within days of the radio broadcast, newspapers all over the country pronounced what Eddie had predicted. The country was now in a state of war, not only against the people who bombed us at Pearl Harbor, but against Hitler and his Nazi Party, trying to rid the world of people who didn't look or think the same as them.

All of South Georgia became abuzz with war talk, young men everywhere flooding into army recruiting centers to sign up and go fight the dirty rotten scoundrels who attacked us. James, Earl and Bobby were some of the first young men in their town to volunteer to go serve. Tommy, a few months shy of his eighteenth birthday, promised his momma he would wait until then to sign up, but sign up he would. Eddie was proud of his boys and not likely to try and dissuade them from serving. It's exactly what he would've done, and coincidentally, exactly what he did do the last time his country needed its brave young men to defend the homeland. He also knew it would be a waste of time to try and talk them out of it. His boys were patriots. Something they got from their father.

Like most other moms preparing to send their sons off to war, Emma became racked with fear and trepidation at the prospect of her four sons traveling to some far away land to fight a war against mad men wanting to take over the world. In front of her sons, she appeared calm, displaying only pride at their willingness to go fight.

"I'm so proud of you boys," she told them more than once.

But inside, she had become a complete mess, and understandably so. As the day neared for her three eldest sons to leave for boot camp (Tommy would follow three months later), it was getting harder for Emma to keep her emotions in check. After supper one night, she excused herself, telling her family she wanted to go for a walk, just to get some fresh air. Eddie and the four boys knew she was having a hard time, despite her outward display of calm. She needed a moment to herself, and they were more than happy to oblige her.

Waiting until she had gotten far enough away from the house where no one inside could hear her, Emma burst into tears, releasing weeks of emotional torment she had kept repressed and hidden from her family. She had never cried like this before in her life. Her apron, crushed into her face, became soaked with her tears and did little to muffle the guttural cries coming from somewhere deep in her soul.

Dropping first to her knees, Emma fell forward, laying herself prostrate on the ground, arms and legs spread wide. She was in a state of complete surrender, complete submission, crying out to God for a way to get through this.

"Please, Father God, I can't get through this on my own," she prayed, sobbing uncontrollably. "My boys mean everything in the world to me. I don't think I could make it through life without them. Please, God, I'm begging you. Protect them. Keep them safe. If you want one of us, I pray you'll take me, just keep my boys safe." The last line added in case the Almighty became amenable to such a negotiation.

Rolling over on her back, she looked up into the heavens, at the thousands of stars twinkling on this clear, cool night. She wanted to look God straight in the face. Thinking back on all the times she sat beside the fire, reading her Bible and praying for guidance or comfort, or whatever happened to be on her plate at the time, she began to recall Bible verses she felt were appropriate for her current time of need.

"Weeping may endure for a night, but joy comes in the morning;"

"He heals the brokenhearted and binds up their wounds," passages from the book of Psalms.

"Blessed are those who mourn, for they will be comforted;"

"Come to me, all you who labor and are heavy laden, and I will give you rest," passages from the book of Matthew.

The Bible verse most appropriate for her at this time was one she learned as a little girl, having relied on it many times in her life. She needed it now more than ever.

"Father, if thou be willing, remove this cup from me; nevertheless, not my will, but thine be done," from the book of Luke.

Emma had been a godly woman for most of her life, ever since she got *saved* at the Catoma Street Church of Christ in Montgomery, so many years earlier. She hadn't always lived a godly life, at least not by what she believed were God's standards. Lord knows she had said, thought or done things in her life she wasn't proud of, but right now she hoped God would overlook those moments of failure and weakness. *He is, after all, a forgiving God,* she thought. Her deep and abiding faith had sustained her in the past, and she counted on it now more than ever, to sustain her again.

She was confident it would, because she wholeheartedly believed in the awesomeness of her heavenly father. She knew God wanted what was best for His children, and she desperately hoped her wishes and God's wishes were equally aligned. Having made her peace, Emma got up to rejoin her family.

Smiling at his wife as she came through the door, Eddie got up from his chair, walked across the floor and put his arms around Emma. Her four sons did the same. It was a touching moment and display of unconditional love for a mother and wife, whose mere presence on this earth had greatly contributed to the man her husband was, and the men her four sons had become.

"Everything's going to be all right," Emma assured her family, smiling through the tears still flowing down her cheeks. With a wink and a nod at Eddie, she added, "I have it on good authority."

CHAPTER NINE

Goin' Cattywampus, I Reckon

Spring of 1942 rolled around, and with it came Tom's eighteenth birthday. With his three older brothers already serving their country somewhere in the European Theatre, taking part in the Allied forces' attempt to defeat Hitler and the Nazi aggression, Tom Franks boarded a train in Valdosta, Georgia, bound for a Marine training camp in San Diego, California. Standing on the platform at the railway depot, Tom wrapped his arms around his mother, doing her best to hold back the tears welling up inside. Unlike his three older brothers serving in the Army, Tom had signed up to be a Marine, wanting to be just like his dad. As proud as any father could be, Eddie shook his son's hand, proclaiming his pride at the man his youngest son had become.

"Always remember, son, listen to your commanders and follow their orders," Eddie advised him. "And never let down your fellow soldiers. You must always rely on each other. It's the only chance you will have to get through this alive. I have complete faith you are up to the task and will not fail. Your mother and I are counting on it."

Tom stared deeply into his father's eyes as he received this final bit of advice. He knew his dad was more than adequately equipped to give such advice, well aware of his father's service during the last *Great War*. Being the youngest of four brothers, Tom never quite felt his status in the world measured up to his older siblings. The words from his father at this moment, however, seemed to provide him with a new perspective. He was now a man; every bit the equal of his older brothers, and the words spoken to him by his dad and hero confirmed it.

As the steam whistle of the train blew, indicating its imminent departure, Tom leaned out the window of his car for one last touch of his mother's hand. Standing perilously close to the automotive as its giant steel wheels began to roll, Emma could not bear the thought of letting go of her youngest son's hand, knowing the length of her separation from him bound to follow. But let go she did. She and Eddie stood still on the platform, waving continuously until the caboose of the train became a small dot on the horizon. Their faith in the Almighty would be tested like never before. Although unsaid by either, they both wondered when and if they would see their boys again.

It took three full days for the train carrying Tom Franks to make it across the country, stopping at various train depots along the way to pick up new passengers. The Marine training barracks in San Diego would be his home for the next five weeks and he was anxious to get there and start this new chapter in his life. Tom barely slept the entire trip, so enthralled by the sights he saw from the window of his train car.

Having never ventured outside the confines of the tri-county area in South Georgia where he had been born and raised, Tom was in constant awe of the vastness of America, having no idea before this moment how big it really was. His quiet thoughts were on his farm back home, his mom and dad he left behind, and his older brothers off in a far-away land already at war. Whispering a prayer for their safety, he wondered if they had seen battle yet. He also thought longingly of Amos, his best friend and companion for most of his life.

At thirteen years old, Amos had become quite old for a dog, especially a large one, and Tommy knew he had probably seen him for the last time. Tommy never left Amos' side the last few days he was home. He was at peace over leaving him behind, knowing his momma loved him nearly as much as he did and would take care of him to the very end.

Several other Marine recruits, on their way to California for basic training, were picked up all along the train's route. Mike Rich, a nineteen-year-old African American Cajun boy from Hammond, Louisiana, got on board when the train stopped at the depot near his home. As most of the passengers already on board were white, Mike began looking up the aisle for an empty row, aware of the current mores of the day regarding the feelings of many whites towards members of his race.

"Hey," remarked Tom, as Mike stood still in the aisle, not finding an empty row where he could take his seat. "I got room by me."

Hesitating for a moment, fully aware of the discerning looks now pointed Tom's way by some of the other passengers, Mike tossed his canvass rucksack in the bin above Tom's seat and sat down beside him. It only took Mike a moment to realize his new seatmate couldn't care less about the color of his skin.

"Hi, my name's Mike Rich," he said to Tom as he offered his hand before sitting down. "My friends call me Richie."

"Tommy Franks," Tom replied, reaching out to shake his hand. "Pleasure to meet you. Where you headed?"

"On my way to California to get trained as a Marine," Richie replied. "Gonna go fight the Jap bastards what bombed us a few months back. How 'bout you?"

"Same here," Tom answered. "I'm from Georgia myself. You from here in Louisiana?" he asked.

"Born and bred right here in Cajun country," Richie replied. "I hope like hell they know how to fix gumbo in California. If not, I might end up wasting away," he added with a laugh.

A year older than Tom, Mike Rich had married his life-long sweetheart, Melissa, three weeks before shipping out. A month after kissing her new husband goodbye on the train platform in Hammond, Melissa discovered she had become pregnant with their first child. She planned on writing him every day and couldn't wait to tell him the news of his impending fatherhood; news he would ultimately receive months later on a remote island in the Pacific Ocean.

As they got to better know each other on their trip, Richie showed Tommy a picture of Melissa, telling him how she insisted on getting married right away. He wanted to wait until he got back home, but like most men in these situations, deferred to the wishes of his beloved.

"She wouldn't say it, but I think she got worried I might not make it back home," he told Tom. "I guess it makes sense. Anyways, she wanted to get hitched, so we did."

They hit it off from the very beginning, especially when Tom talked about Amos and how hard it was to leave him behind.

"A Catahoula?" Richie remarked when Tom told him about his life-long best friend. "You know he's a Cajun dog, don't you? I got two of 'em myself."

A special friendship had been forged at this very moment. They talked about each other's families, friends, their hometowns where they grew up; anything and everything to take their minds off the reason they sat beside each other on this very train.

When they finally pulled into the station in San Diego, an olive drab green bus awaited their arrival, with men in crisply pressed Marine uniforms standing beside it, shouting out the names of the new recruits they had come to pick up. When Tom and Richie heard their names called, they boarded the bus and took their seats together. The world they both had known their entire lives was about to undergo a drastic change. The next five weeks would turn these two young country boys into killing machines.

"The damn Japs ain't never gonna know what hit 'em," Richie remarked with a smile, as their bus drove through the gates of their new temporary home.

***

At eighteen years old, Tom Franks had already become a full-grown man, standing six feet tall and weighing a little over one hundred and ninety pounds. At the conclusion of his five weeks of basic training, he had put on about ten pounds of muscle and was a solid piece of granite. Much to their surprise, he and Richie had somehow survived the training and were now proud members of an elite fighting force, anxious to join their fellow soldiers in the war against Imperial Japan.

As their basic training neared conclusion, word spread throughout the base of the U.S. victory in the *Battle of Midway,* Japan's first significant defeat by American forces since Pearl Harbor. Excited at hearing the news and elated over successfully completing their arduous basic training, the morale of the newest Marines was sky high. They couldn't wait to receive their deployment orders and begin doing their part in defeating the hated Japanese.

Men who have been in battle can never adequately explain what it's like to someone who hasn't. Tom had listened to story after story from his dad about his experiences in battle; but would never be able to fully appreciate what he went through until he experienced it for himself. An experience which would not take him long to fulfill.

A month before the *Battle of Midway,* Japanese forces had occupied a small group of islands in the South Pacific known as the Solomon Islands. From this vantage point, they planned on launching attacks on Allied forces in the Pacific, causing a disruption in supply lines and communication routes between the U.S., Australia and New Zealand. Allied commanders, fully aware of the importance of denying the Japanese a foothold on these islands, began working on an operational plan to attack the islands and force the Japanese to retreat.

Operation Watchtower, planned for implementation later in the summer, would be the first major offensive against Japan by Allied forces, requiring a wave of U.S. Marines to assault the Solomon Islands of Guadalcanal, Tulagi and Florida. The objective of the plan was to kill as many Japanese soldiers as possible and deny them control of these strategic islands.

Tom and Richie sat beside each other on a Navy landing craft, as it cut through the waves and approached Guadalcanal at the commencement of their amphibious assault on the island. Their mission, an attack on enemy forces controlling the only airstrip on the island, had been designed to wrestle control of the airstrip from Japanese soldiers and force them to retreat into the jungles.

All the Marines, including Tom and Richie, were scared and apprehensive as they approached shore, ducking to avoid rifle fire coming their way as their boat skidded to a stop in the sand. Tom and Richie hurdled the fallen bodies of fellow Marines, lying dead on the ground, as they ran from their boat in seek of cover.

Because of their need to move quickly, the supplies carried in their rucksacks were kept to a minimum. Food had to be rationed and soldiers were limited to only two meals per day. Several weeks would pass before supply lines could be established and food and other supplies could be adequately replenished.

Like many of his fellow Marines, Tom contracted a case of dysentery, which zapped him of well-needed energy and strength. Although he had a rough go of it, in the end, Tom performed his duties in a manner his father would have been proud of.

After months of intense fighting, the mission Tom and Richie participated in ultimately proved successful, as control of the islands fell into the hands of the Allies. The Japanese, not easily deterred, mounted counter attacks over the next few months to retake the islands, resulting in massive casualties on both sides. Tom had seen death up close and personal and had narrowly escaped his own demise on several occasions, most notably with the help of his friend Richie.

As part of a 25-man patrol sent out on a reconnaissance mission, Tom and Richie quietly made their way through the woods in search of a small group of Japanese soldiers who had supposedly indicated a desire to surrender.

Instead of encountering enemy forces with their hands raised, the patrol group Tom and Richie were in walked into an ambush. The patrol commander immediately shouted an order to retreat, as shots rang out, mowing down several of the Marines. Firing at the enemy as he attempted to retreat, Tom tripped and fell as a Japanese soldier chased after him from behind. When he rolled over and attempted to stand, Tom looked up, staring into the eyes of his adversary who hovered over him with the bayonet on the end of his rifle perched above his head.

In a moment of immediate clarity, Tom realized his death was imminent. Before he could react, however, his attacker's skull exploded, shot through the head from behind by Richie, who, after seeing Tom fall, ran over to assist him. Richie continued running in Tom's direction and helped him to his feet, as both young Marines continued their retreat.

Of the twenty-five men taking part on this reconnaissance mission, only six made it back alive, including Tom and Richie. It was Tom's first brush with certain death, an experience he would not soon forget. Nor would he ever forget Richie's act of bravery, which most assuredly saved his life.

Tom loved getting letters from home, a treat he and his fellow Marines enjoyed on an irregular basis, since the ships and planes delivering supplies to their tiny Pacific island showed up only sporadically. Sometimes Tom would get one or two letters, then nothing for a few weeks, followed by a dozen or so at one time, once another mail sack arrived. His mom's letters were the only way he could keep up with how his older brothers were doing, and the only way his brothers could keep track of him.

Richie walked into the tent he and Tom shared, only to find Tom sitting on the edge of his bunk, letter in hand, looking dejected. He immediately realized Tom had received bad news from home.

"What's up brother?" he asked, placing his hand on Tom's shoulder out of obvious concern.

"It's Amos," Tom replied. "Mom told me some time ago he had been spending more and more time just lying on the front porch, not wanting to do much of anything. He's pretty old, so I guess I expected this. Mom said she came out to bring him his supper one night and he just lay there. Wouldn't eat anything. She covered him with a blanket and went back inside to go to bed. The next morning when she went outside to check on him, he was dead. Just plum gave out sometime during the night."

"That's awful, man," Richie replied. "I'm really sorry, Tom. I know how much you loved him."

"What about you?" Tom said, not wanting to dwell on Amos. "Did Melissa finally have that kid of yours?"

A smile beamed across Richie's face as he reached into his pocket and pulled out his letter from his wife. Inside the letter, he removed a picture of a beautiful eight-pound baby boy.

"Meet Michael Alex Rich, junior," Richie said, handing the picture to Tom. "We're gonna call him *Alex*."

"Dang," remarked Tom, "he's a good-looking little fella. Thank God he took after Melissa and not your ugly butt!"

"Gimme the picture back you son-of-a-gun!" Richie said with a laugh, placing it back inside Melissa's letter.

It was a nice moment between the two friends. The loss of Amos, while not a surprise, would be tough for Tom to get over, as he knew it would. The joy of sharing with his best friend the birth of his newborn son was certainly a salve on the wound to his heart, as the sadness over losing Amos became instantly mitigated by the delight over the birth of Richie's son.

Almost six months after U.S. Marines came ashore in the Solomon Islands, defeating the Japanese forces, the Allied victory seemed to be secure, despite several counterattacks by the Japanese. The Japanese hierarchy in Rabaul (located on the Pacific island of Papa New Guinea, their command headquarters) decided to make one last attempt at retaking the airstrip they had lost in the *Battle of Guadalcanal*. By doing so, the Japanese concluded they would be able to fly in massive amounts of supplies, armaments and additional forces to mount a counteroffensive against the Allies and reestablish their stronghold in the Pacific.

Low on supplies, men and morale, the Japanese army cobbled together every last man, in a desperate attempt to defeat the U.S. Marines in control of the airfield. When they suddenly appeared from the woods surrounding the airstrip, the Japanese soldiers ran towards the Americans, firing their weapons and tossing grenades as they advanced. From behind makeshift bunkers, fortified with sandbags, the Marines returned fire, mowing down the seemingly endless wave of desperate Japanese fighters. One by one they fell, until finally the assault had been completely repelled. When it ended, the bodies of hundreds of dead Japanese soldiers littered the landscape.

Tom came out from behind his bunker and looked to find Richie, to make sure he was okay. Running over to where he knew his friend had been positioned when the assault began, Tom peered over the wall of sandbags forming Richie's bunker, and found Richie on the ground, rifle still in hand. Apparently, a random grenade tossed by one of the charging Japanese soldiers, had somehow managed to land in Richie's bunker, exploding before Richie had a chance to grab it and toss it safely away. Riddled with shrapnel wounds and bleeding from multiple places on his body, Richie laid perfectly still, his eyes cold and open.

Tom immediately began shouting for a medic, jumping up and down and waving his arms for someone to come and help. Instinctively, though, he knew his friend was dead. Dropping to his knees in front of Richie's body, Tom wrapped his arms around his friend and buried his face in his chest. He could not hold back his tears and made no attempt to even try. His best friend, the man who had saved his life a few short months before, had been killed. As he looked into his best friend's lifeless face, Tom thought of Alex and how sad it was Richie would never get the chance to hold his son or watch him grow up; and how Alex would be robbed of the joy of knowing his father. Tom had never felt such pain before in his life and wondered how anyone had the capacity to withstand it. Unfortunately, more pain would surely come, and it would be the kind of pain capable of shaking his very foundation.

CHAPTER TEN

Heavens to Betsy

<u>Morven, Georgia, 1943:</u>

Emma walked inside the house carrying a bucket of water she had drawn from the well outside to wash the dirty dishes left over from breakfast. Her kitchen table had been strewn with tomatoes, corn and collard greens, all part of the lunch menu she would begin preparing as soon as she got her dishes cleaned. The two iron skillets on top of her stove would soon be filled with biscuit dough and ham hocks.

Since there weren't any hungry, growing boys at home to feed, Eddie and Emma usually had just two meals a day; a good strong breakfast to start the day, and a late lunch after Eddie had put some work in out in his fields. She would always leave some leftovers on top of the stove if Eddie wanted a little snack before going to bed.

As she got ready to light the firewood in her stove to cook lunch, Emma heard the sound of car tires rolling over the gravel in their driveway and come to a stop. Way too early for lunch, she figured Eddie had forgotten something and had come back to the house to get it. After hearing two car doors slam shut, she dismissed the idea of it being Eddie and assumed someone had come by for a visit. After wiping her hands on the front of her apron, she untied the apron string in back and slipped her apron over her head, hanging it over the back of a chair before walking over to the front window.

A cold chill coursed through her veins the moment she saw two men in military uniforms standing beside their car, straightening their hats and making sure their shirts were properly tucked. One of the men carried with him a leather attaché case. On the side of their vehicle Emma noticed some sort of emblem with the words *U.S. Army* emblazoned below. Eddie, having been inside his tool shed several yards away, also heard the sound of the vehicle when it arrived and had begun walking back towards the house as the men exited their car.

Emma nervously opened her front door and stepped out onto the front porch as the men approached. Stopping at the bottom of the front porch steps, the first man removed his hat before speaking.

"Ma'am, my name is Captain Bill Huse, and this is Sergeant Williams," he began, as the second man in uniform also removed his hat. "Is this the Franks home, ma'am?"

"Yes, it is," Emma replied, barely able to respond. "I'm Emma Franks and this is my husband, Eddie," she continued, pointing behind the men to Eddie who had walked up beside the two military men.

"Captain Huse, Sergeant Williams, I'm Eddie Franks," Eddie remarked, extending his hand to greet the two visitors.

"It's a pleasure to meet you, Mr. Franks," the captain replied. "May we come inside and talk?"

Eddie escorted the men up the steps and onto the porch, before leading them inside the house. Emma was still frozen in place as Eddie got beside her and placed his arm around her waist, nudging her to follow the men inside.

"Emma, I'm sure these men are a little parched," Eddie said. "Would you be so kind as to pour them a glass of iced tea? Please gentlemen, have a seat," he continued, as he motioned them to the chairs slid under their kitchen table. "May we offer you something to drink?"

"We'd be much obliged, thank you," Captain Huse replied, as he and Sergeant Williams sat down, placing their hats on the table near the tomatoes.

Emma began moving in slow motion, not fully aware of what was happening around her. She instinctively knew, as Eddie most certainly did, the visit to their home from uniformed military men could only be to deliver news about one of their sons.

"May I ask the nature of your visit, Captain Huse?" asked Eddie, not wanting to prolong the suspense any further.

Emma stood still beside the table, glass tea pitcher in hand, awaiting the answer to her husband's question. She had stopped breathing for a moment, unaware her face had turned ashen from lack of blood and oxygen.

"Mr. and Mrs. Franks," the captain began, "I'm afraid to tell you we have disturbing news to report about your son James. He has been killed in battle. It happened a little over three weeks ago. Apparently…"

Before the captain could finish his next sentence, the glass pitcher in Emma's hands crashed on the floor, shattering in a million pieces, splashing iced tea everywhere. Eddie rushed to her side and grabbed onto her before she had a chance to fall, her knees buckling from beneath her as she became faint. Sergeant

Williams jumped up and slid his chair over behind Emma so she could sit down. Captain Huse, who also rose to render aid, gently placed his hand on Emma's shoulder and helped Eddie guide her into the seat. The captain allowed a few moments to pass before attempting to continue.

The tears had not yet begun to flow, most likely because Emma and Eddie were in a state of shock, wanting to hear some kind of explanation about what had happened to their oldest son.

"Mr. and Mrs. Franks, it grieves me deeply to be the one to deliver this news to you," Captain Huse continued, now looking at Eddie. "The commander of all U.S. military forces, General George C. Marshall, has asked me to deliver a letter to you explaining everything about what happened to Sergeant Franks and how he died. Garrett, may I have the letter," he said, turning his attention to Sergeant Williams, who had already begun reaching for the manila envelope contained inside his attaché case.

As the sergeant handed the envelope to Eddie, the captain continued. "Your son died a hero, Mr. and Mrs. Franks, and on behalf of myself, Sergeant Williams, and every other person in uniform, I want to personally thank you for his service and sacrifice."

Turning to look at Emma, Captain Huse knelt down in front of her and placed both hands on the sides of her shoulders and added, "And to you and your husband, Mrs. Franks, we owe a debt of gratitude for your sacrifice as well. Thank you."

The captain and sergeant retrieved their hats and shook Eddie's hand before departing, as Emma leaned forward in her chair and began weeping into her hands. Keeping his emotions in check, at least for the time being, Eddie looked at the envelope in his hand, placed it on the table before him, and knelt beside his wife, pulling her into his bosom.

With a sudden calmness only her faith in an Almighty God could provide, she whispered through her tears, "Read the letter Eddie."

Carefully opening the envelope so not to tear the letter inside, Eddie removed the contents. After noticing the heading on the letter indicating it came from "The War Department," Eddie began to read out loud.

Dear Mr. and Mrs. Franks,

It is with great sympathy and a heavy heart, I must inform you of the death of your son, Sergeant First Class James Franks. As an important member of a B-17 Bomber crew, your son, along with all ten members of his flight crew, perished over the skies of France while bravely performing their duties in defense of the Allied efforts to defeat Nazi Germany.

As the mission on which your son lost his life was part of a secret campaign in our war efforts against the Nazi oppressors, I cannot provide any more specific details about his passing. But rest assured, your son died a hero, and his sacrifice, and the sacrifice of other young men like him, will ultimately help usher the United States to victory over the evil forces we are engaged against, and bring this nightmare of war to an end.

On behalf of President Roosevelt, I would like to express my condolences over the loss of your son. The entire United States military, whom I represent, and a grateful nation, are in your debt. May God provide you peace and comfort in this trying time. I am…

Some years later, Eddie and Emma would learn the details of the mission on which their son had been killed. While on a routine surveillance mission over northern France, an American pilot flying a Douglas A-20 Havoc took pictures of construction sites in the French town of Amiens, where the German army was in the process of building missile launch pads. Allied commanders feared the sites would be used to launch missiles carrying chemical and biological warheads, presenting an existential threat to Allied forces and the thousands of French citizens living in the region.

Operation Crossbow, a secret tactical operation designed to obliterate the missile sites with an overwhelming bombing campaign, was subsequently initiated. After unloading a bay full of 1000-pound bombs on the site, the B-17 bomber (known as the *Flying Fortress),* on which James served, had been struck by anti-aircraft fire and crashed, leaving no survivors. James, as well as the entire crew, was posthumously awarded the Silver Star for heroism.

*****

Tom sat motionless reading the letter from his mother, detailing the events surrounding the heroic death of his brother James. His heart ached over the thought of losing his hero and protector, but it broke over the thought of what his mom must be feeling. He wanted more than anything to be able to put his arms around her and give her comfort, assure her things will be okay. *How were Earl and Bobby handling the news,* he thought.

Tom longed for a return to the simpler times of life on his farm, running through the woods with Amos and being harassed by his older brothers. Although it had been barely a year since saying goodbye to his mom and dad on the train platform in Valdosta, it seemed like a lifetime ago for Tom.

Self-preservation for his own sake no longer became his top priority. He had to make it through this war so his momma could see him again, unable to fathom the depth of despair his sainted mother would have to endure if another of her sons failed to make it home alive. Suddenly regretful of all the times he disappointed her; backtalking her or lying to her over some stupid thing he did; he wanted nothing more than to look her in the eyes and tell her how much he loved her. His father too, of course, but the thought of his mother consumed him now.

The several hundred surviving Japanese soldiers on Guadalcanal and the rest of the Solomon Islands were eventually shipped off to POW camps in Australia. After surviving six months of intense fighting during *Operation Watchtower,* Tom's daily routine became fairly innocuous. With the Japanese threat in the Solomon Islands totally defeated, the Allies fortified the islands with additional personnel and armaments and began using the islands as a base from where assaults on the Imperial Army of Japan were launched. The war in the Pacific had begun to turn in favor of the Allies, and Tom's contributions to the effort were not insignificant.

As the end of 1944 approached, the Japanese army was in total retreat, their defeat in World War II all but certain. Earl and Bobby, who had both participated in the D-Day landings in France earlier in the year, were on the move towards Germany as Allied efforts to defeat Hitler and the Nazis were progressing favorably. Tom allowed himself to believe he might actually make it out alive and would soon return home to his parents and the life he once knew.

Tom knew the Japanese army would fight to the very end, unwilling to surrender even if their hopes of victory were all but vanquished. He had personally witnessed this level of resolve and had no illusions of final victory coming easily.

In March of 1945, American General Curtis LeMay led a devastating aerial assault on Tokyo, firebombing the city and killing thousands of its citizens, in hopes of convincing the Japanese Emperor surrender was his only option. Unfortunately, it took the dropping of two atomic bombs on Hiroshima and Nagasaki a few months later before he finally ceded to the wishes of the Allies and agreed to surrender.

Prior to the dropping of the bombs, which effectively ended the war in the Pacific, some of the Marines in the Solomon Islands, including Tom, were withdrawn and sent on another mission. Thousands of American prisoners of war being held at *Camp O'Donnel*, a Japanese POW camp in the Philippines, were going to have to be liberated once the Allied victory over Japan was complete. American generals feared the Japanese guards at *Camp O'Donnel* would assassinate the prisoners once victory became imminent and wanted to get a group of Marines there to prevent such a massacre from occurring.

Three years earlier, after the Japanese army secured the surrender of American and Filipino forces trying to defend the Philippines from Japanese aggression, more than seventy thousand prisoners were captured. What followed was a human atrocity known as *The Bataan Death March,* where the prisoners were marched more than sixty miles, without food or water, to *Camp O'Donnel,* many of them tortured and murdered along the way. Thousands died during the march, including five to six hundred American GIs. Thousands more would die over the next three years awaiting rescue, enduring unimaginable treatment at the hands of their captors.

By the time Tom and his fellow Marines reached the gates of *Camp O'Donnel*, the Japanese surrender had been secured, ending the war in the Pacific Theater. Rifles were stacked along the fences surrounding the camp, left there by the Japanese guards who got word of the surrender and fled the premises. Thankfully, none of them felt the need to shoot their prisoners before departing, although nearly a third would die within the next year due to the maltreatment received while incarcerated.

The first American prisoner Tom encountered happened to be a young soldier, perhaps twenty-five or twenty-six years old. He looked fifty and weighed no more than eighty pounds. Tom immediately unscrewed the cap on his canteen and began pouring small sips of water into his mouth, cradling the man like a small child. Within minutes, dozens more surrounded Tom, longing for a sip of their own. As his canteen of water passed from man to man, Tom removed some packets of water crackers from his pocket, broke off small pieces, and passed them around as well. With stomachs so shriveled from years of starvation, the men could barely swallow more than a bite or two.

My God, he thought, *how could this have happened!* His hatred for his Japanese adversaries only intensified.

The Japanese general in charge of the soldiers responsible for the atrocities was eventually tried as a war criminal and executed. The sight of tortured, emaciated fellow soldiers would haunt Tom's dreams for the rest of his life. Like many who served in battle during the war, Tom went home with an innate understanding of the existence of evil in the world and the need for good people, and good nations, to defeat it.

CHAPTER ELEVEN

Lawd Have Mercy

Several of Tom's family members were resting comfortably in the waiting room, while others were away resuming the normalcy of their daily lives. Some were at work; others shopping for groceries; a few were ushering Tom's great grandchildren to and from school. A visitor, unrecognized by any of the Franks family members in the room, appeared in the doorway and asked about Pop's condition.

Tom's daughter Karen, the only one of his three children present, got up to meet the visitor.

"Hi, I'm Karen, Tom's daughter," she said by way of introduction, extending her hand to shake his. "I don't believe we've had the pleasure."

"My name is Thomas Rich," he replied, smiling back at Karen and making eye contact with the others present. "I drove over from Baton Rouge this morning to see about your father. How's he doing?"

"He's resting comfortably right now," Karen replied. "We're hoping to get in and see him shortly. The doctor thinks he may wake up sometime today and we'll have a chance to speak to him. Forgive me, but how do you know my father?"

"Actually, I don't really know your father," Thomas replied. "I met him once, about thirty-five years ago when I was ten. Your mother and father were driving through Louisiana and stopped in to visit with my dad. I would have brought him along, but his health is not too good, and the drive over would've been pretty tough on him. Lord knows he wanted to come, though."

"Oh my gosh," Karen remarked, suddenly realizing who this visitor was. "Your dad is Alex Rich."

"Yes ma'am, he is," Thomas replied. "Your dad and my dad have been speaking by phone a couple of times a year. Been doing so for as long as I can remember. They spoke a few weeks ago and your dad mentioned his health seemed to be in decline. After my dad tried calling him at home for the past few days and couldn't reach him, I phoned the hospital to see if he was here. Once they told me he had been admitted, I came right over."

"I'm so glad you did, Thomas," Karen said. "We're waiting for the doctor to come by with an update, so in the meantime, grab a cup of coffee and sit with us. I want to hear about your father."

"Thanks, I will," he replied.

One of Karen's nieces, completely unaware of the connection, introduced herself to Thomas and asked how his father knew Pop.

"Actually, it's my grandfather who was most connected to Mr. Franks, having served with him in World War II. Right after my grandfather joined the military, and prior to him leaving to go serve, he and my grandmother decided to get married. They had been childhood sweethearts, and them ending up married had always been the plan."

"Turns out, my grandmother got pregnant with my father and didn't know about the baby until long after my grandfather had shipped out. A few months after my dad was born, she received word from the military my grandfather had been killed in action while fighting somewhere in the Pacific."

"Apparently, after Mr. Franks came home from the war, he looked in on my grandmother from time to time, making sure she was okay. My dad always told me he did it out of loyalty to my grandfather."

"You know, my dad hardly ever talked about the war when we were growing up," Karen said. "We gave him his space because we assumed he had seen some awful things and never wanted to relive them. I do recall, though, every Christmas there would always be a present or two under the tree with the name *Alex* on it. My dad told us he was the son of a special friend of his who lost his life in the war. He didn't like to talk about it and we never really asked him to. I do know his friend's name was *Richie,* and he saved my father's life over in the war."

"Yeah, it's pretty much the way I heard it as well," replied Thomas. "Anyways, my grandmother never remarried, so my dad grew up without a father in the home. They were in Louisiana and your dad lived here in Georgia, so he couldn't really be around much, but I think he tried to be a good influence on my dad. I know he sent my grandmother money from time to time. Not a lot, but enough to help. When my dad got ready to graduate from high school, your dad drove over to see him and told my grandmother he wanted to pay for my dad to go to college."

Shocked at hearing the news, Karen remarked, "Now there's something I didn't know! So, my dad put your dad through college?"

"Yes, he did," answered Thomas. "My dad graduated from LSU in Baton Rouge, stayed around for graduate school, and ended up getting a teaching position there. He taught at the school for forty years before retiring a couple of years ago. I followed in my dad's footsteps, also becoming a professor at LSU. I've been there about eighteen years myself. None of which would have been possible without your dad's help."

Dear Jesus, Karen thought, *I never knew.*

***

<u>Valdosta, Georgia, 1945:</u>

Standing arm in arm with his mom and dad, Tom waited on the train platform in Valdosta as the big steam engine pulled into the station and slowed to a stop. Emma's face, already soaked with tears in anticipation of Earl and Bobby's arrival, began beaming when her two boys stepped from the train and began running in their direction. Acutely aware this family reunion was incomplete with the absence of James; they were all elated at being together once again. Even Eddie, his fiftieth birthday behind him, had softened considerably and had to dab some tears from his eyes. After hugging and kissing their mom, Earl and Bobby both wrapped their arms around Tom's neck, pulling him close and giving him a giant bear hug.

Slapping him hard between his shoulder blades, Earl remarked, "Dang, Tommy, you put on a little beef since the last time we saw you."

Indeed, he had. Tom, smiling broadly at his two older brothers, stood a full inch above both, and outweighed them by at least ten pounds. With a muscular and chiseled frame, Tom was no longer anyone's *little* brother.

"I guess we're done pickin' on you," remarked Bobby with a laugh, grabbing him by the arm and pretending to punch him in the chest.

The disconnect between the brothers caused by the years spent apart seemed to fade away almost immediately. In no time, they were traipsing through the woods together on their farm; swinging from tree limbs; splashing around in the river; and wrestling with one another on the front porch, much to the chagrin of their mother.

"Take it into the yard, boys," she would tell them. "By golly, you're gonna tear the house down."

Seldom mentioned, the absence of James was a huge void and everybody knew it. Emma had long ago made peace with God over his loss and wanted only to concentrate on showering her three remaining sons with all the love she could muster. Mad at God for the longest while, Emma believed He had somehow let her down by taking from her their firstborn. In the end, however, she simply concluded James had been so special and unique; God needed him up there more than He needed him on earth. It became the only way she could cope with his loss. At times, she received comfort by the thought of James being in heaven looking down and watching over them.

After helping their father get through a season of planting and harvesting tobacco crops, Earl, Bobby and Tom all wanted to take some time off away from their farm. Prior to being shipped off to fight in the war, the boys had barely ever wandered more than a few miles outside the boundaries of Brooks County. Now, having experienced travel to all parts of the globe as soldiers in the United States military, their tiny little town in South Georgia seemed almost microscopic. Earl and Bobby wanted to drive over and see the Atlantic Ocean, drink beer on the beach and chase skimpily clad girls in bathing suits. Tom, however, had more noble intentions.

"I want to drive over and meet Richie's wife and son," he told Emma. "I've got a little bit of money saved and I want them to have it. It's the least I can do."

Emma could not have been prouder of the person her youngest son had become. Her heart ached for Melissa and Alex after Tom told her the story of how Richie saved his life. As a mother herself, Emma could only imagine how tough it must be for a young mother to raise a son without his father around.

"I think it's a great idea, Tom," Emma replied. "I believe it's exactly what Richie would've done for you."

***

When Old Man Jenkins died the previous year, Emma and Eddie visited his daughter and grandchildren on their farm to pay respects to a man they considered like family.

"I swanee Eddie, my daddy had never been sick a day in his life," his daughter commented. "He just plum gave out. Worked his self to death, I reckon."

Mid-sixties was way too young for someone to just "plum give out," but men back then didn't seem to last as long as they should. A lifetime of consuming bacon, pork chops and buttermilk biscuits with thick, rich gravy, probably contributed to this fact more than hard work.

A basket-load of fresh picked vegetables was placed down on the Jenkins' kitchen table, as Emma embraced each of the children with genuine, heartfelt sympathy.

"I'm happy to sit up with him tonight," Eddie offered, because that is exactly what family members did for those who passed.

"I'd be honored," his daughter replied. "Not sure my daddy would put up with anybody else, Eddie," she added with a smile. "Come outside with me, Eddie, there's something I want to show you."

Eddie and Mr. Jenkins' daughter walked outside, stopping beside the old man's 1934 Ford Model BB pickup truck. In virtually mint condition, the truck had barely 10,000 miles on it, having never been driven farther than fifty miles from where it sat.

"My daddy loved this truck, Eddie, and he took really good care of it," she said. "I ain't got no use for it and can't drive it anyhow. I can't think of anyone my daddy would want this truck to go to more than you. I know your three boys are back home now, and I'm sure one of them could make good use of it. I want you to have it, and I won't take no for an answer."

Touched by her sincere act of kindness, Eddie graciously accepted her gift, promising to always keep the truck in its present pristine condition.

When Tom mentioned he wanted to drive over to Louisiana and visit Richie's family, Eddie offered up Mr. Jenkins' truck for the trip.

"No sense letting it sit in the garage collecting dust," Eddie said, who never wanted to use the truck on his farm anyways, concerned the wear and tear would negate his promise to Old Man Jenkins' daughter.

Tom took his time on his drive over to Hammond, Louisiana, where Richie's wife and son lived, stopping along the roadside to nap in his truck whenever he grew tired. He bonded with Alex almost immediately upon his arrival at their home. Almost four years old, Alex reminded Tom so much of Richie as he held the young boy in his arms and looked into his face.

"You got your daddy's eyes," he told Alex, as Melissa looked on and smiled.

Tom and Melissa stayed up late each night talking about Richie, recounting story after story of the time they both spent with him. The void left in Melissa's heart by Richie's death would never be filled, but she received great comfort from Tom, who seemed to love him almost as much as she did.

"He saved my life, Melissa. I feel I owe him," Tom said. "I'm not sure I'll ever be able to repay him, but I want to try. If it's okay with you, I'd like to check in on you and Alex every now and then. I think it's what Richie would want me to do."

"Of course, Tom, you are always welcome here," Melissa said through tears, as she embraced Tom before he left. "Thank you so much for coming. It means more than you'll ever know."

His expression to Melissa of his desire to help them out and be a part of Alex's life was not a pledge Tom would ever take lightly. For the rest of Tom's life, Richie, Melissa and Alex would occupy a special place in his heart, even if the depths of such devotion he would find difficult to share.

As he made his way across Louisiana, into Mississippi, and across the Alabama state line, Tom decided he was in no real hurry to get back home. A couple of extra days on the road wouldn't hurt anyone, he figured, and a slight detour, he felt, might be in order. He knew his mother had been born and raised in Montgomery, but remembered very little of the city, having only visited there two or three times as a youngster. When he got to Dothan, Alabama, he turned his truck north, with the intention of spending the night in Montgomery. As fate would have it, he never made it quite that far.

CHAPTER TWELVE

Sweet Tea and Fried Okra

<u>Troy, Alabama, 1946:</u>

Paved highways across the state of Alabama were few and far between, and Tom found the only one within fifty miles, heading north from Dothan. Thanks to something known as *eminent domain,* the road on which Tom travelled cut through large swaths of privately owned farmland, as far as the eye could see on both sides of the highway. Acres upon acres of corn, soybeans and cotton filled Tom's view as he gazed out the windows of his truck while he drove. *Amber waves of grain,* a line he had sung a million times from *America the Beautiful*, immediately came to mind. *I had no idea Alabama was so beautiful,* he thought.

When he passed the city limit sign for Troy, Alabama, he decided to pull off and grab some lunch. As he pulled his truck to a stop in front of *Miss Blossoms' Schoolhouse Restaurant,* the smell of a pig, spit-roasting on a massive wood-fire grill out front, filled his nostrils, triggering an instant reaction in his salivary glands. *Now this should be good,* he thought, as he walked through the door of the restaurant.

"Just grab a seat anywhere," a waitress behind the counter shouted, "I'll be right with you."

He slid a chair out and took a seat at a table next to where three men were seated enjoying their lunch. "Hello," he said, politely addressing the men before sitting down. They nodded in return as Tom looked over the menu before him.

"What can I get you to drink?" the waitress asked, after placing a basket of piping hot corn muffins on the table in front of Tom.

"Sweet tea, ma'am, and a large plate of barbeque," he answered. "I could smell it from a mile away."

"Good choice," she replied. "You want some fried okra on the side?"

"You bet I do," Tom answered with a smile, as he handed her his menu.

"Comin' right up," she said before walking away. "I'll be right back with your tea."

While waiting for his drink to arrive, Tom grabbed a muffin and smeared a slab of butter on top before taking a bite. As he listened to the conversation going on between the three men near him, he determined they had recently come home after serving in the war. Like military veterans of this, or any other war, he immediately felt a kindred spirit with them and leaned back in his chair to speak to them.

"I take it you guys all spent some time in the war?" he began. "I had three brothers who served in Europe, while I got to go fight the Japs in the Pacific."

Smiling at hearing this, the men reached out to shake hands with Tom and introduced themselves.

"Why don't you come join us," one of the men said to Tom, after the introductions concluded.

"Don't mind if I do," Tom replied as he got up and changed seats, bringing with him his basket of muffins.

"We all spent our time in Europe," the first man said. "Pretty brutal, really. We were just talking about how glad we are to be out of there. I'm sure you had it pretty rough as well. I heard those Japs could be real savages. How bad did it get for you?"

"No worse or better than what you guys went through," Tom replied. "I was with the Marines when we invaded Guadalcanal, some God-forsaken island in the Pacific. The whole time we were there it was so hot we might as well have been living in an oven. Can't tell you how nasty those Japs were. I hate to tell you, but *savage* is too nice a word for them. I saw firsthand what they did to the American POWs. I only wish we had dropped another two or three atom bombs on them before calling it quits. I'm sure the Nazis you guys had to deal with were just as bad."

"Yeah, they sure were," replied the second man. "We all lost buddies over there. How 'bout you, did you lose anybody close?"

"My best friend Richie saved my life on the island. Shot a Jap soldier through the back of the head right before he was about to run his bayonet through my chest. A couple of months later we were holding off a whole mass of them coming at us when a grenade landed in his bunker. Don't think he ever knew what hit 'em. I got to him right away, but it was too late. Nothin' I could do to help him."

"My oldest brother James was killed in France," Tom continued, looking down at his feet as he recalled the death of his brother. "He flew on a B-17 and got shot down while on a bombing mission over there. None of his crew survived."

"Geez, man, I'm so sorry to hear about that."

"Yeah, thanks," Tom said. "My other two other brothers made it back okay, though. They both served under Patton in the Seventh Army. Got to go into Sicily and help capture Palermo and Messina. They almost had a chance to go after Hitler, but the son-of-a-gun ended up killing himself. They're back home in Georgia now, where I'm from. What about y'all? You from around here?"

"Two of us are," the first man replied. "Went to high school together in Goshen, a little town not far from here. As soon as the war broke out, we skedaddled over to the recruiting station and signed up. The ugly guy on the end over there," he continued, pointing to third man, "is from North Carolina. We all served together in the same unit. Believe me, we're glad to be back home."

"I hear ya, man," Tom replied. "What about you?" Tom asked, looking at the guy from out-of-state. "What brings you here?"

Happy to change the subject from the dire consequences of the war they all shared, the man from North Carolina explained the three of them had just finished signing up for classes at the local college.

"The G.I. Bill, man, it's free money," he told Tom. "Can't pass it up."

Tom had never heard of the G.I. Bill and had no idea what his new friend was even talking about.

The Servicemen's Readjustment Act of 1944 (or *G.I. Bill*), signed by President Roosevelt, was a way to pay benefits to returning servicemen by funding their college tuition. Tom wanted to know more.

"Troy State Teacher's College is only about two miles from here," Tom was told. "You should at least take a drive by and look at the campus, it's really beautiful. Not to mention all the co-eds walking around, studying to become teachers," the man added with a grin.

"You know it," his friend chimed in with a smile. "They don't look like any of the teachers I had when I went to school."

"So, you guys are gonna become teachers?" Tom asked.

"Just me," the first man answered. "These guys aren't sure what they want to be yet," he added, smiling at them. "The college is mainly for training teachers, but they have other programs as well."

"The main thing, it's free tuition," Tom was told with emphasis. "Who knows how long the government is going to offer it. They told me about the college because they live close by," the North Carolinian explained, pointing to his two friends. "I figured I'd drive over and check it out, and so far, I like what I've seen. You should definitely take a ride over there and check it out for yourself. There's a guy in the office helping vets sign up. He knows everything there is to know about the G.I. Bill and how to get them to pay for everything."

Tom had never given college much thought...until this very moment. Although his original plan had been to continue driving north to visit his mother's hometown of Montgomery, he figured it couldn't hurt to make another slight detour. His new friends had piqued his interest, and he wanted to find out for himself if what they had told him was true. Although a minor detour with regards to his originally scheduled trip, it would become a major one in terms of redirecting his entire life.

***

At this point in Tom Franks' life, he had only done two things… farming and fighting in a war. Since the curriculum at Troy State Teacher's College had nothing related to war, and since he had no desire to become a teacher, he signed up for classes related to the only thing he really knew anything about…agriculture. The college offered a degree program in something called *The Business of Agriculture,* and Tom decided it sounded like something he might be interested in.

When Tom eventually made it back home and told his family about his desire to go to college, the news was not met favorably by his dad nor his brothers.

"What in tar nation you want to go to college for?" Eddie remarked, clearly planning on Tom joining him, Earl and Bobby in the running of their family farm. "There's work for you to do here, son, and wasting time going to college ain't nothin' but a fool's errand."

"Yeah," chimed in Earl, "you expect me and Bobby to carry your load?"

"But daddy, you don't understand. There's things I can learn in college that can help us in the long run. I don't see it as a waste of time. I really think it will pay off for all of us down the road."

Nobody in his family had ever stepped foot on a college campus before and Eddie was not interested in seeing his youngest child start a new tradition, especially when there was plenty for him to do within the family business. Emma, however, had a slightly different take.

"You do what you think the good Lord wants you to do," she advised him later when they were alone. "You have to be true to your calling, no matter what me, your daddy or your brothers think. It's your decision, and yours alone to make. Just be sure you believe it's what God wants you to do. You pray about it and then stick by your decision."

"I have, momma. I just wish daddy could see I'm trying to better myself and not think I'm running out on him."

Caressing Tom's face with the palms of her hands, Emma gently kissed her youngest son on the forehead.

"Your dad will see it in time, Tommy. Just be patient with him."

"I hope you're right, momma. And thanks," Tom replied, standing to give his beloved mother a proper hug. "I could always count on you being in my corner."

"Well, that's not likely to change anytime soon, Tommy. And don't fret about daddy. I can promise you he's in your corner too. It just might take him a little longer to show it."

Although clearly disappointed by Tom's decision, Eddie nonetheless attempted to show support for him (no doubt at the behest of his wife) as Tom departed his family home and headed off to college. While he certainly felt some regrets, he was convinced the path he had carved out for himself was exactly where he needed to go.

Although the G.I. Bill covered all his school fees, Tom still needed extra money to pay for his living and entertainment expenses, the latter becoming more prevalent once he discovered the beer hall located a mile from campus.

One day, while walking to class in Bibb Graves Hall, he spotted a "Help Wanted" ad pinned to a bulletin board in the hallway, offering ten dollars a day for help tending to horses at a local horse farm in neighboring Luverne, Alabama. He snatched the notice from the wall and put it in his pocket before continuing to class, not wanting anyone else to see it and get to the farm before him.

First thing the following morning, Tom got in his truck and headed straight for the *Duke Family Horse Farm* in Luverne, for what he hoped would be a successful job interview.

A massive sign bearing the *Duke* name, and a large etching of their family crest met Tom as he drove through the front gate and onto the property. The farm, six hundred acres of beautiful rolling hills and grassy pastures, had a long, paved driveway leading to the house, lined on both sides with century-old pecan trees. A dozen workers, some with long poles designed to grab the limbs and shake loose the bounty of nuts ripened for harvest, were collecting the pecans in large burlap sacks strewn over their shoulders. A few politely waved at Tom as he passed.

Upon reaching the house, Tom parked his truck to get out and was greeted by Mr. Duke's foreman, Robin Boutwell.

"Good morning, sir, my name's Tom Franks," Tom said, reaching out to shake Mr. Boutwell's hand. "I'm here about the job tending to your horses. I go to school over at Troy State and I found this ad on one of the bulletin boards," he added, removing the crumpled-up piece of paper from his pocket and handing it to the foreman.

"I'm Robin Boutwell," the foreman replied. "I kinda run things around here for Mr. Duke. Let's walk over to the barn and I'll show you the horses and we can talk about the job. I never woulda' pegged you as a college boy. You from around here?"

"Not exactly, sir," Tom replied. "I grew up in South Georgia, in a little town called Morven. I spent a couple years as a Marine during the war and came home last year. I happened to be on my way to Montgomery, where my momma grew up and got sidetracked when I came through Troy. Decided to use some of the G.I. Bill money and go to school."

"Don't much blame ya," Mr. Boutwell said, "it's a pretty good deal for you guys. We didn't get squat when we came home from the First World War."

"Yeah, I know. My daddy served there as well."

"What does he do now?" Mr. Boutwell asked.

"We've got a farm back home," Tom answered. "Mostly tobacco, but my dad and my brothers will also grow some peas, soybeans and occasionally an acre or two of corn."

"My older brother had a pretty big spread south of here," Mr. Boutwell continued. "Close to two hundred acres. Made a ton a money growing tobacco. After he died, he left the farm to my nephew, his only child. His lamebrain kid went and sold the land so he could buy a racecar. Can you believe it? What an idiot. Lives down in Florida somewhere near the beach. A damn shame I tell you."

"Makes no sense to me," Tom offered, trying to sound agreeable to the man he hoped would become his new boss.

Mr. Duke's foreman liked Tom from the very beginning and hoped he would take the job once he found out what it entailed. Arriving at the door of the horse barn, he pushed it open, and the two men went inside.

"Dang, Mr. Boutwell, you guys call this a barn?" asked Tom as he looked around, amazed at how pristine it appeared. "I've been in a lot of barns in my life, and I ain't never seen one quite like this."

At sixty-five hundred square feet, the barn was equipped with twenty individual horse stalls, each twelve feet by twelve feet in size. In addition to the stalls, the barn had a large horse shower, and a tool shed three times bigger than the one Tom's dad had back home. Beautifully finished oak wood molding outlined each stall, with wrought iron gates attached to the openings. The floors of each stall were made of dirt, with six inches of hay for padding so the horses would be comfortable when they lay down. Finely polished brick pavers covered the center walkway, which ran the length of the barn from front door to back.

"Good Lord, I've never seen anything like this before," Tom commented as he looked around in awe of the barn's magnificence.

"Yeah, Mr. Duke doesn't do anything halfway," Mr. Boutwell said. "If you take the job, I'm gonna want you to be in charge of keeping this place as nice and clean as you see it now. Calvin is the guy, what takes care of looking out for the horses, so you won't need to worry about them too much. He'll probably want you to feed 'em from time to time, maybe cool 'em off after they been run, but primarily your job is gonna be to make sure this place stays clean. So, what do ya think, you want the job?"

"Yes sir, I definitely want the job Mr. Boutwell," Tom replied. "If you don't mind me asking, what does he do with all these horses?"

"First off, everyone around here calls me *Bout*. Not Mr. Boutwell and definitely not Robin, just *Bout*. As far as these horses are concerned, only a couple of them belong to Mr. Duke. The one on the end…his name is Shadow. Be sure you clean his stall first every time you come in, and make sure there's plenty of hay on the floor for comfort. Shadow belongs to Miss Jackie… Mr. Duke's daughter."

"Most of the horses we see come through here belong to people who keep 'em here before they get ready to race 'em. They'll stay with us until racing season begins and then they'll ship 'em off all over the country to different tracks. Them people got a lot of money invested in these horses and Mr. Duke ain't very happy if they're not being properly cared for. You're taking the place of a guy I fired last week 'cause Mr. Duke found an empty feed bag on the floor of one of the stalls."

"Gotcha," Tom said, suddenly wondering if his decision to apply for this job was a smart one.

"The pay's ten dollars a day" Tom was reminded, "and since you're gonna be in school most days, you can show up every day after you get out of class. Four or five hours a day should be plenty to get done what you need to get done. Not too bad money for half-a-day's work."

"No, not at all," Tom remarked. "I'm looking forward to it. When do you want me to start?"

"Since we're already at the end of the week, let's start Monday afternoon," Bout answered, as he closed the barn door and prepared to walk Tom back to his truck.

"Sounds good," Tom remarked. "I'll see you Monday afternoon."

Tom drove back to the one-room apartment next to the Troy State campus he leased for fifteen dollars a month, excited about starting his new job. No way could he know, however, how his new job would forever alter the rest of his life in a most positive way.

CHAPTER THIRTEEN

Pretty as a Peach

The work was pretty much as Bout had explained it, and three days into his new job Tom had settled into a regular routine. First thing after arriving at the Duke farm, Tom made sure to clean Shadow's stall, which included scooping up and getting rid of any of the horse's *droppings* left behind since the previous cleaning. All the other stalls were then similarly tended to, followed by a trip to the hay barn where Tom would load thirty or forty bales onto the hay wagon and drive the tractor into the barn. Once inside, he cleaned out the soiled straw on the floor of each stall and replaced it with fresh hay, making sure to provide a thick, cushy pad of comfort for each horse.

One day, after returning from an afternoon ride, Jackie Duke rode Shadow into the barn to put him up for the night. As Tom finished putting away some tools into the tool shed, he stepped out onto the brick floor of the barn as Shadow passed by, unaware Jackie had entered the barn. The sudden appearance of Tom onto the floor of the barn in front of Shadow startled the horse, causing him to rear backwards, raising both front legs into the air. Jackie let out a scream as she tightened her grip on the reins and tried to stay upright on her horse.

"Whoa, whoa," Tom said to the horse as he reached up and took hold of Shadow's reins.

As Shadow's front legs settled back onto the floor, Tom gently petted the side of Shadow's face as the horse began to calm down, much to his relief. Tom turned his attention to Jackie, who had been as startled as her horse when Tom appeared in front of them.

"Are you okay, ma'am?" he asked, unable to hide his embarrassment for almost causing Jackie to fall.

"Yes, thank you," Jackie answered, as she dismounted while Tom maintained his grip on Shadow's reins.

"You gave me quite a scare," she added, as she took the reins from Tom and began walking Shadow to his stall.

"Yes ma'am, I'm sorry about that," he politely responded. "I didn't hear you come in. Are you sure you're alright?"

"I think I'll live," Jackie replied, finally able to smile. "You must be the new guy Bout told me about." Extending her hand to shake his, she continued. "I'm Jackie Duke, pleased to meet you."

"Tom Franks, ma'am, it's a pleasure to meet you."

After Shadow had been secured in his stall, Tom and Jackie exchanged small talk for the next twenty minutes, or so. As he looked into her eyes while she spoke, Tom suddenly became conscious of his increased heart rate and how much he needed to repeatedly wipe his sweaty palms on the front of his shirt. He couldn't remember ever seeing a woman so beautiful. Although Tom tried hiding the nervousness in his voice when he spoke, it did not escape Jackie's notice. She was flattered by the obvious effect she seemed to have on Tom but did not want to do or say anything to add to his torment. She thanked him for helping her with Shadow and excused herself to return to the house. Not wanting Tom to see the broad smile on her face as she walked away, Jackie kept her head pointed in the direction of her house, while suddenly realizing the palms of her hands had become unusually moist.

He's a hired hand, she reminded herself, shaking her head to remove any thoughts of attraction she may have been feeling. Jackie thought Tom was perhaps the most handsome man she had ever met, but it was ridiculous for her to think anything would ever come of it. She shuttered at the thought of what her daddy would do if she ever became involved with someone like Tom. Jackie did not, however, know her father as well as she thought she did.

***

Having recently celebrated her twentieth birthday, Jackie Duke had been an only child and the apple of her daddy's eyes. Her mother had died giving birth to her, and her father never found good reason to remarry. Compared to most others who lived in Pike County, Alabama, Roy Duke was a relatively wealthy man, who dedicated his life to the upbringing of his daughter, intent on providing for her a life he never had as a child growing up during the *Depression.*

One of the most respected men in town, Roy had been a founding member of the Luverne Golf and Country Club, an exclusive and private resort for some of the men in the area with a few extra bucks to spend. The club, whose membership was all male and all white, once hosted the U.S. Amateur Golf Championship. Even the great Bobby Jones, who had retired from competitive golf some years earlier, made frequent trips from his home in Atlanta to play the course.

Jackie, like all other women, was not allowed on the golf course, but was a frequent guest in the club's dining room. A welcomed addition to a room usually filled with older, sweaty men who had been golfing in the hot sun for four or five hours, Jackie was universally loved. Particular on the list of admirers was Lyle Duff, the son of another of the club's founding members and the brother of Nancy Duff, one of Jackie's closest friends. Lyle and Jackie had been dating for several months, and while Jackie did not consider theirs a serious relationship, Lyle thought otherwise.

Several times over the months following their initial meeting, Tom and Jackie exchanged pleasantries whenever they ran into each other, usually in or around the horse barn. Some of the meetings, which most would consider random, were actually calculated encounters by Jackie, who often found reasons to visit Shadow when she knew Tom would be in the barn. Careful not to let on how much she enjoyed Tom's company, Jackie thoroughly liked the way she felt whenever she and Tom were together.

***

Temperatures neared a hundred degrees one July afternoon, as the hot sun beat down on Tom as he pulled the tractor to a stop outside of the horse barn. A wagonload of hay bales, neatly stacked on the trailer behind the tractor, were waiting for Tom to move them inside. Before beginning, he removed his shirt, already soaked with sweat, tossed it on the seat of the tractor, and walked over to a 50-gallon wooden barrel filled with water, which sat beside a well pump near the barn. After gulping down several mouthfuls of water to quench his thirst, Tom continued to dip the metal ladle into the barrel and pour the cool water over the top of his head, letting it run down his neck, back and chest, providing him with welcome relief from the suffocating heat.

Partially hidden behind the drapes in her bedroom, Jackie peered out her window at Tom standing beside the barn. The muscles in his arms and chest, taut and massive from months of lifting eighty-pound bales of hay, glistened as the afternoon sun reflected off the water running down his body. She was barely conscious of the outside world, as she stood frozen in place, her gaze trained on Tom's figure down below. Only the sound of a car pulling to a stop outside her window caused her to snap out of her self-induced daze. Lyle and Nancy Duff, and another friend, Rita, had come by for a visit. Jackie ran downstairs and walked out on her front porch to meet her friends.

Roy Duke, having heard the car arrive, came around from the side of the house and met them as well.

"Hey Mr. Duke," Lyle said, ignoring Jackie for a moment so he could go suck up to her dad.

Roy greeted his visitors and invited Lyle to come around back with him to show him something he had been working on.

"Sure thing, Mr. D," Lyle replied, moving in his direction. Looking back at Jackie standing on the porch, he added, "Jackie, how 'bout running some iced tea out to your dad and me. Thanks sweetie."

"Why of course, *sweetie*," she quietly said, not loud enough for anyone to hear. A long eye roll accompanied her words, which were dripping with sarcasm.

Nancy and Rita joined Jackie on the porch, as the men disappeared behind the house.

"How is it, your brother is always more interested in impressing my dad than he is me?" Jackie asked Nancy.

"He's a man, Jackie, just deal with it," Rita interjected.

Before going inside, Rita looked over towards the barn and noticed Tom unloading the bales of hay.

"Oh my God," remarked Rita. "Who in heaven's name is your new farmhand over there?"

"Damn, Jackie," added Nancy. "When did you guys hire him?" "Yeah, Jackie, you little tramp," Rita said playfully. "Something tells me you've been hiding him from us."

"Okay, knock it off you two," answered Jackie, rolling her eyes at her two friends. "You sound absolutely ridiculous, for crying out loud. His name is Tom and he's a very nice guy; been working here for the past few months."

After delivering two large glasses of iced tea to her dad and Lyle, Jackie returned inside the house to Nancy and Rita.

"Hey Jackie, Nancy and I want to go out and see Shadow," Rita said, with a sly look and smile in Nancy's direction.

"Yeah, I bet you do," Jackie replied, as she followed her friends out the front door, already halfway to the barn.

When the ladies reached the door to the barn, Tom was nowhere to be found. Rita and Nancy walked over to Shadow's stall and began petting the horse's head, all the while looking around to see where Tom had gone.

"Damn, girls, look like we missed him," Rita said, with obvious disappointment in her tone. "I wanted to get a good look at him up close."

"Me too," added Nancy. "I think I might want more than just an up-close look…if you know what I mean," she said, as she and Rita laughed out loud.

Although the conversation between her two best friends made her a bit uncomfortable, Jackie did her best to hide it from them.

"I'm telling you right now, Jackie," Rita began, taking the conversation further into the gutter, "nobody would blame you if you went slummin'. If I was you, I'd take him over to your daddy's hay barn and have me one helluva romp."

Nancy and Rita burst out laughing, as Jackie smiled awkwardly. She forced herself to laugh but turned her head away so her friends could not see the discomfort on her face.

"Well, I'm not so sure my brother Lyle would approve," remarked Nancy, still laughing. Poking Jackie in the side with her finger to get a reaction, she continued. "But don't worry, I won't say a thing."

"Yeah, Jackie, we know how to keep a secret," added Rita, as she and Nancy laughed even louder.

Jackie, again, forced herself to laugh while hiding her obvious discomfort.

As they walked back to the house, Jackie felt regret for not calling her friends to task for their intemperate remarks. She tried her best to change the subject, but her friends were having too much fun. As they reached the front porch of the house, Tom quietly stepped out of the tool shed inside the barn, where he had been standing throughout the entire ordeal. Not wanting Jackie or her friends to know he had overheard their conversation, he waited a long time before eventually taking the tractor back to the hay barn where it belonged and calling it a day. The words stung, but hearing Jackie laugh along with her imprudent friends hurt him deeply.

CHAPTER FOURTEEN

Wore Slap Out

With horse racing season in full swing, the stables at the Duke farm were empty, except for Shadow and one other family horse. The lack of need for his services was fine with Tom, having become less enthusiastic about showing up for work since the incident in the barn with Jackie and her friends. He told Bout he needed to get ready for exams and asked if he could come in just once a week for the next little while. Not a complete lie, as exams actually were coming, but the real truth had been he feared running into Jackie. She made him nervous enough as it was and definitely didn't want to encounter her with this other thing hanging over their heads.

"No problem," replied Bout. "You do whatever you need to do not to flunk out of school. I don't want to lose you. Me and Calvin can handle things when you're not here."

***

<u>Morven, Georgia, 1947:</u>

Perhaps due to his father's reproach about his college plans, Tom felt some degree of skepticism early on about how much a degree in *Business Agriculture* would actually benefit his family farm back home. However, as he got more into the program, he began to realize there were many aspects of it, if properly implemented, which could actually help to improve profits.

Increased investment in farm machinery and some of the newer

130

agriculture chemicals on the market would result in much higher crop yields on the backside, substantially driving up profits. He also considered how more efficient use of their land, including adding crops like peanuts and grapes to their yearly crop rotations, could also increase their bottom line and improve the overall condition of their soil.

Even animal husbandry, something his father had never previously considered, could prove very profitable for their family business. Raising chickens for eggs, or cows for milk and meat were areas he wanted to pursue with his dad and brothers when he got back home.

After completing his first year of college, Tom came home for summer break to pitch in and help with chores around the farm. He also had a longing for his momma's cooking. While he loved most of the food in Alabama, especially the barbeque, his momma's hog jowl stew with collard greens and crumbled up corn pone tossed in, was simply unequaled.

Earl and Bobby, anticipating starting families of their own in the future, decided to build their own homes on some unused pastureland near their parent's house. They were glad Tom had come home to help them with their project.

"Well, you don't look any smarter," said Earl, as the brothers sat down for supper.

"Give 'em time, Earl," added Bobby. "He's still got a couple of years to go."

Emma looked across the table at Eddie and smiled; happy her family was together again.

"I've been thinking about driving over to *Campground* after supper and visiting James," Tom said to his mom. "Maybe put some fresh flowers on his grave."

"I think it's a wonderful idea," Emma replied. "Why don't we all go, it'd be nice to go see him as a family. I think he'd appreciate seeing us all show up."

The next morning, Emma had a hearty breakfast prepared for her men before they started their workday.

"Let's go boys, we're burnin' daylight," Eddie said to his three boys as he headed out the door. "Them houses ain't gonna build themselves."

Three-foot high walls of cinder block formed the foundations of Earl and Bobby's new homes. A large band saw Earl had bought from a local lumberyard sat equidistant between the two structures. After chopping down some White Oaks and Pines from their property, the boys hauled the fallen trees over to where Eddie manned the saw, turning the trees into boards used for framing the homes. Once the framing had been completed, it came time to put the roof on.

"You don't need to go up there, daddy," Bobby said to his father, as Eddie leaned his ladder against the framed structure and began to climb.

"Like heck I don't," he replied. "You want this done right, don't you?"

The three brothers looked at each other, knowing it would be useless to try and argue.

"Okay dad, just let me get up there with you and give you a hand," Tom said, sliding his hammer in his waistband and following his father up the ladder.

Earl and Bobby stayed on the ground below, handing up sheets of plywood for Tom and Eddie to nail in place to form the roof.

In between the sounds of their hammers pounding in nails, Eddie had a chance to catch up with his youngest son on what he had going on in his life; how he liked school; if he had *met* anyone. He tried to keep his comments positive and not turn things negative by rehashing their disagreement about Tom's decision to go to college instead of dedicating himself to the family business. The tension had not entirely subsided, and Tom could feel it. Certain as ever of the propriety of his decision, Tom tried convincing his father of all the benefits he was receiving from his education. He soon realized this effort was in vain and abandoned it.

"I've pretty much been concentrating on school and work," he told his dad. "Been working for this fellow who owns a big horse farm. Haulin' hay and tending to his horses. Some other odd jobs here and there. Pays me decent, enough to have a little spending money on the weekends."

"What the heck do you know about horses?" Eddie asked, his question dripping with sarcasm.

"Not much, except they crap a lot," Tom answered, trying to cut the tension with a little levity.

Tom thought of Jackie, of course, but didn't mention her. No reason, really, to do so. He didn't figure there was much chance anything would ever come of it, no how.

"Well, I know you don't want to hear this, but we could sure use you around here," Eddie continued, setting his hammer down and looking Tom square in his face. "But I reckon you're a man now, and you gotta make your own decisions."

"That's all I'm trying to do, dad," Tom replied with an element of chagrin in his voice he could not subdue.

"Stop your yakkin' up there," Bobby shouted, holding up a piece of plywood for his brother to grab, "we got work to do."

"Yeah, yeah, yeah, stop your bellyaching," Tom replied as he reached for the next sheet of wood to hammer in place.

As Tom pulled the piece of plywood up through the rafters and slid it in place, he heard Earl shout, "Watch out!" as Eddie's hammer fell from the roof and landed on the ground beside Bobby. Tom looked over at his dad who stared back at him, kneeling on one knee and clutching his chest. The look on his father's face was ominous.

"Dad, are you okay?" Tom shouted, quickly sliding his body across the top of the unfinished roof to reach his father.

"I'm not feelin' so good all of a sudden, Tommy. I think I may have over did it this time."

"Earl, Bobby, get up here," Tom shouted to his brothers. "Something's wrong with dad."

They raced up the ladder to help Tom with their dad, who by now had become unconscious, laying across a set of rafters.

"We're going to have to tote him down," said Earl. "Bobby, stay on the ladder and I'll slide him down to you. Tommy, grab his legs and pull him towards me and then climb down and get behind Bobby on the ladder."

The brothers worked together and got their father down off the roof without any of them falling. After laying him in the back seat of their truck, Earl got behind the wheel and drove to the house, stopping for only a minute so Tom could jump out and get their mother. Seconds later they were screaming down Coffee Road on their way to the hospital in Valdosta. For the entire drive, Tom kept his face buried in his hands, wondering if he had contributed to his father's condition.

It took Earl less than twenty minutes to make it to the hospital. For the entire drive, Emma held Eddie's head in her lap, looking into his face as she stroked his hair. Quietly singing the worship hymn, *In the Sweet By and By,* the smile never left her face, as streams of tears rolled off her cheeks. The calmness in their mother's demeanor provided comfort to Earl, Bobby and Tom, who otherwise were in a state of panic. Somehow, she just knew.

"In the sweet by and by, we shall meet on that beautiful shore."

Emma kept singing the line over and over again, until Earl pulled the truck to a stop at the hospital. Attendants ran out to help and rushed Eddie inside. Within minutes, however, as Emma and her sons stood at Eddie's side, the doctor slowly removed the stethoscope from his ears and placed a comforting hand on Emma's shoulders.

"I'm sorry ma'am, but he's gone."

The pews in Mt. Zion United Methodist Church can comfortably accommodate about a hundred and fifty people. Folding chairs increase the number by another forty, or so. As Eddie's body lay in repose in his flag-draped casket at the front of the church, nearly three hundred people made it inside, many standing three and four deep against the walls of the church. At least two hundred more were outside, all wanting to pay their last respects to a man they considered a pillar of their community.

Emma and her sons sat in the front pew listening to the preacher deliver his sermon, extolling the virtues of Eddie and reminding everyone how much this man meant to all of them. With her face buried in Tom's chest, ten-year-old cousin Dot sat in his lap, quietly weeping throughout the service.

"Greater love hath no man than this, that a man lay down his life for his friends," the preacher began. "The Scriptures tell us this, and it's the way Eddie Franks lived his life. He risked his life for all of us when he went overseas and fought in the *Great War.* But when he came home, he wasn't through fighting, was he? Right here, in our own community, he fought against racism and bigotry, and he made this a better place to live. Who in here hasn't been helped by Eddie in some way or another? Very few I reckon."

The entire room became one big *Amen Corner* as shouts of affirmation to the words of the preacher rang out.

The preacher continued. "The Bible also tells us to judge a man by his fruits; by the works of his hand; what kind of legacy did he leave behind. As I look down at his beautiful wife Emma, and their three sons, Earl, Bobby and Tom, I see a great legacy.

And we can't forget their oldest boy, James, who two days ago met his father at the Pearly Gates and welcomed him home. My goodness," the preacher continued, his own voice beginning to shake, "how beautiful a reunion they must've had."

Emma smiled through her tears, acknowledging the touching words from their pastor, as those seated around her reached forward and gently squeezed her shoulders. It had been a beautiful service, one befitting a man so loved and respected by everyone who knew him.

Enough food to feed an army awaited the people who had come to bury Eddie and celebrate his life with Emma and her sons. They all wanted to see Emma and squeeze her hand or hug her neck, just to let her know how much Eddie meant to them. They loved her as well. Emma was revered like few others in this little town.

Emma, Earl, Bobby and Tom stood for hours after the service until every person there had a chance to express their feelings to each of them. The outpouring of love and emotion meant a lot to Emma and was something she would never forget.

"I think I should stay momma, and not go back to school," Tom told his mom after returning home from the funeral, still feeling some guilt over the passing of his father. "You're gonna need me around here now that daddy's gone."

"Nonsense, Tommy," his mom replied. "Now you know I'd love to have you with me, but you need to go back and finish your schooling. Anyways, Earl and Bobby have been pretty much running things around here for a while. They can get done what needs doin'. You concentrate on your studies. We ain't never had anyone in this family go to college, much less graduate. I'm countin' on you being the first."

"She's right, Tommy," Earl added. "As much as me and Bobby would love to see your ugly face around here, you oughta go back and finish up what you started. I know daddy never warmed to the notion of you going to college, but he only wanted what was best for you. For all of us. I think he would agree you ought not to quit now."

"I reckon," replied Tom. "If you're sure you don't need me."

"We didn't say we don't need you, Tommy," Bobby began, as a smile formed on his face. "We're sayin' we don't want you," he finished, poking him in the ribs with his elbow.

"Spoken like a true brother," said Emma, reaching her arms out for a well-needed hug from her sons.

CHAPTER FIFTEEN

Fixin' to Open Up a Can of Whoop-Ass

Tom Franks' two youngest great grandchildren, Ava and Brayden, shrieked with delight when Dot Edwards walked into the hospital waiting room, accompanied by her granddaughter. The four-hour drive had been exhausting for Dot, but the sight of her family, coupled with the display of exuberance by Ava and Brayden, instantly renewed her strength and vitality.

"Miss Dot!" the children screamed, running across the room and launching themselves into her waiting arms.

"Kids! Let Miss Dot sit down," Karen implored her two grandchildren, afraid their physical assault might knock her to the ground.

"Nonsense," Miss Dot replied, returning their very appreciated hug.

As everyone else present got up from their chairs to greet her, Dot smiled, obviously happy to be in the presence of her beloved family.

"I've been waiting four hours for this hug."

Dot's extended family returned the love she had for all of them in spades. The yearly Franks family reunion at *Campground*, which Dot has coordinated each year for more than three decades, is always well attended and a highlight of everyone's summer. Besides the

Sunday service at Mt. Zion, followed by a picnic on the grounds near the cemetery, the festivities every year begin with a Saturday night gathering at *Ray's Mill Pond Restaurant,* where fried catfish, hush puppies and cheese grits are consumed in abundance.

Following supper, the children (not to mention some of the adults) love to go out on the deck of the restaurant and toss bits of hush puppies to the waiting mouths of alligators floating in the pond outside, many of whom seem to know when reunion weekend has arrived. After lunch on Sunday, before everyone heads out of town and back home from where they came, the weekend concludes with a mandatory stop at *Lawson's Peach Stand* for a basket of fresh peaches and a large bowl of homemade peach or blueberry ice cream.

Planning this reunion every year is what sustains Miss Dot and has probably added a decade to her life. Some of her younger kin who live in the area have been volunteering for years to take over the duties of putting the weekend together, but have been rebuffed at every turn. It's what she lives for.

Tom Jr., on his way back from his father's room, heard the commotion coming from the waiting room and rightfully assumed Miss Dot had arrived.

"I'm so glad you made it, Miss Dot," he said, greeting her with a hug. "You must be tired. Can I get you something to drink?

"Maybe in a minute," she replied. "How's your daddy?"

"I just came from seeing him. He's doing as well as can be expected. No change, really. He's still comfortably sleeping. We're waiting for him to wake up so we can talk to him. Hopefully it won't be much longer."

"Can I go in and see him?" Dot asked.

"Of course, you can," Tom Jr. answered. "I can walk you over right now if you like. If anyone can get him to wake up, it's probably you."

As she stood by his bedside and looked into his face, a lifetime of memories flashed by in Dot's mind, like a movie being projected on a large silver screen. Everything came rushing back, beginning with her earliest memories of playing with Tommy and Amos on their farm in Morven. She recalled saying goodbye to him when he left to go off and fight in a war she had been too young to understand, and how happy she became when he finally came home years later. She remembered when cousin Emma invited her family down for Sunday supper to meet Jackie for the first time, and all the times she babysat for them following the births of Tom Jr., Jim and Karen.

She smiled when she thought about the time she once told him she would never forgive him for moving his family to Newnan, knowing full well she neither meant it, nor did he believe her.

One thing Dot Edwards had little doubt about: the world had become a better place for having Tom Franks in it and would be a lesser place when he left it.

***

<u>Troy, Alabama, 1948:</u>

Tom had calculated if he took a few extra classes and bore down on his studies, he could complete his four-year degree in only three. With his father now gone, he wanted to get home and put his degree to work, helping his brothers run the farm, and bring with him some new ideas to help grow profits.

Earl and Bobby had not been as adversarial as their father towards Tom for his decision to forgo the farm for college, probably because they realized it wouldn't have been their place to do so. Nonetheless, they never truly approved of their little brother's decision. Their momma, however, was totally committed to providing Tom with as much support and encouragement in his career decision as possible, and Earl and Bobby knew their place. In time, they became placated to the fact Tom was going to finish college, and for their mother's sake, it was best for them to appear agreeable. They weren't about to let little brother come home after a few years away at school and start telling them how to run things but instead, would have an open mind in hearing whatever ideas Tom had regarding the direction of the family business.

In the end, they would come to recognize Tom's talent and intellect, and in no way felt threatened by Tom's desire to bring new ideas and changes to the way they had been running the farm. They also knew it was how their momma wanted it, and after all, Emma was ultimately still in charge.

***

The Front Porch, a local beer hall near the Troy State campus where Tom and some of his friends liked to unwind, had recently installed a television set above the bar to attract more patrons. On a night when the football game between *The Fighting Irish of Notre Dame* and the *Purdue Boilermakers* was scheduled to be broadcast, Tom decided to join his friends there to watch the game.

The Notre Dame squad, considered the best team in college football at the time, was playing in-state rival Purdue, hoping to stage a big upset. Tom knew nothing about football, and in fact, had never been to a game. The Troy State *Red Wave,* as they were known back then, played their football games on a 10-acre site near the campus, but Tom never felt a desire to go see a game.

Upon watching the two teams take the field before the start of the televised game, Tom's comment elicited laughter from his friends, when he said, "Why are there convicts out there?"

"Spoken like a true hillbilly from Georgia," one of his friends replied.

Halfway through the game, the front door opened and in walked Jackie Duke and her friend Nancy Duff, who had agreed to meet Nancy's brother Lyle and two of his friends for a beer. Lyle had gotten to the bar a full hour before Tom, and having secured a table in the back, never noticed Tom sitting at the bar with his friends. Lyle motioned for Nancy and Jackie to join them, after seeing them come through the door.

When Jackie approached their table, Lyle put his arm around her and leaned in towards her face, attempting to kiss her on the lips. Somewhat repulsed by the stench of alcohol on his breath from an hour of hard drinking, Jackie politely turned her face away and instead accepted a kiss on her cheek.

Having spent the summer out of town visiting relatives, Jackie had only recently returned and now felt immediate regret for her decision to accompany Nancy to *The Front Porch*. While not overly excited about Lyle's invitation in the first place, she only agreed to go as a favor to her best friend, who told her she didn't want to go to a bar alone.

"It's not ladylike," Nancy told her.

"Looks like y'all got started without us," Jackie sarcastically remarked to Lyle and his friends, as she looked at Nancy and rolled her eyes.

"Don't worry, you girls got time to catch up," replied Lyle with a laugh.

Since returning to Troy following his dad's funeral, Tom had resumed his work schedule at the Duke horse farm but had not yet seen Jackie because she had been away.

Prior to her and Nancy's arrival at the bar, Tom left his friends at the bar and walked out on the back deck to finish his beer, having lost interest in watching a football game he clearly cared nothing about.

"Hey Jackie, isn't that the gorgeous guy who works for your daddy?" Nancy asked, pointing out the window leading to the back deck.

"Oh my gosh, it sure is," she replied, looking in his direction. "Tom is his name. I'm gonna walk out and say hello."

"Hang on, Jackie," Lyle replied, trying not to sound jealous. "You don't need to go out there, your party is right here. Just drink your beer and let the farmhand alone," he added, smirking at his friends as he spoke.

With a stern look at Lyle noticed by everyone at the table, Jackie replied, "I'm going to go out and say hello. Anyone's welcome to join me."

As she turned and walked away, Lyle's friends looked down and smiled, pretending not to notice the embarrassing look on Lyle's face. After taking a few seconds to let Jackie's words soak in, Lyle felt a sudden urgency to redeem himself in the eyes of his sister and friends. He wasn't about to let his girlfriend defy him, at least not in front of them.

Partly out of anger for Jackie's act of defiance, and partly due to the seven or eight beers he had already consumed, Lyle slammed his glass mug on the table and loudly declared, "Like hell you will."

The remark, while aimed at Jackie, had actually been intended for those still at his table, as Jackie was no longer within earshot. The two friends and Nancy quickly got in line behind Lyle and followed him out back, anticipating an encounter they were sure would take place.

"This oughta be good," one friend remarked.

Jackie and Tom had barely exchanged pleasantries when the back door crashed open and Lyle appeared, obviously upsct.

"Jackie, take your ass back inside like I told you in the first place," exclaimed Lyle.

Having never been spoken to like this by anyone before, Jackie stared back at Lyle, a look of shock clearly on her face.

"Lyle, you're obviously drunk. Go back inside and leave me alone," she responded. "You're being a total jerk right now, and you're embarrassing us both."

Once again, his authority over his girlfriend, which he felt rightly his, had been directly challenged. And it happened in front of his sister, his two friends and several other people on the back deck looking on with interest. His pride, as well as the alcohol coursing through his veins, would not allow him to simply walk away.

Reacting out of sheer anger, he reached out and grabbed Jackie by the back of her hair, yanked her backwards and pushed her into Nancy, standing a few feet away. When Jackie turned back to look at Lyle, contemplating a response to his boorish behavior, he raised his hand above her head, as if he was about to backhand her.

Stopping short of actually striking her, he stared Jackie in the eyes, while telling his sister to, "get her the hell back inside."

As Nancy pulled Jackie away from her brother and out of harm's way, Lyle turned to face Tom, now staring at him with a look of disbelief. With both friends only a few feet away, Lyle felt emboldened, with a sudden urge to exact revenge on someone who clearly had done nothing wrong. It didn't matter. Lyle's pride had taken a massive hit, and he wanted everyone to see him kick this guy's butt.

Under almost any other circumstances, Lyle would never have challenged Tom. However, with the presence of his two friends (whom he assumed had his back) and the copious amount of alcohol in his system providing him with added confidence, he became determined to start a fight and regain the manhood he felt had been taken away from him. It turned out to be a dreadful mistake. Not just for him, but for his two innocent friends as well.

Lyle looked back at his friends and said, "Let's kick his ass, boys."

Although shocked at what they had been witnessing the past minute or two, Lyle's friends, whose judgment had become as impaired as Lyle's, made a snap decision to back their friend. A decision they would soon regret.

Lyle lunged towards Tom and wildly swung his fist in the direction of Tom's face (the only punch he would throw), which Tom easily blocked. In an instant, all of the hand-to-hand combat training he had learned as a Marine came back to him. As he blocked Lyle's punch with his left hand, he immediately followed with a sharp uppercut with his right, catching Lyle under the chin and lifting him off the ground. Lyle's body crashed into the railing surrounding the deck, and before he had time to recover, Tom reached down and grabbed the bottom of Lyle's pants legs, lifted his feet off the ground, and flipped him over the railing into a creek below.

Before his body hit the water, Lyle's friends jumped on Tom's back and tried to wrestle him to the ground. As fast as he had dispensed with Lyle, Tom elbowed one guy in the throat, causing him to fall to the deck, and grabbed the other in a bear hug, lifted him off the ground and deposited him over the railing where he landed on top of Lyle. Before the third guy had a chance to stand, Tom grabbed him with one hand on the back of his shirt collar and the other on the back of his waistband. In one fell swoop, he tossed him over the railing as well, much like tossing a bale of hay into the back of a pickup truck, something he had done thousands of times. The fight, if one could call it a fight, lasted all of fifteen seconds.

Jackie rushed to Tom's side and began apologizing. Looking at her, and then over to Nancy, he recalled the comments he heard in the barn about *going slummin'*, and the laughter which followed, including from Jackie.

"I guess you could call that one helluva a romp, couldn't you?" Tom said to Jackie, with utter disdain in his voice.

As he turned to walk away, Jackie and Nancy stared at each other, both with their hands covering their mouths, a look of sheer embarrassment on both their faces.

Frozen in place for a moment before she was able to move, Jackie looked at Nancy and said, "I'm going home. You can get a ride with your idiot brother."

***

When Robin Boutwell showed up for work the following morning, Jackie greeted him as soon as he drove through the front gate.

"Good morning, Bout."

"Good morning, Miss Jackie. Is everything okay?"

"I need to speak to Tom. You don't happen to know where he lives, do you?"

148

"I'm expecting him later this afternoon, can it wait 'til then?"

"No, it can't, Bout. I really need to talk to him right away."

"He rents a room over on Folmar Street, right next to the campus. It's the little white house with a rope swing in the front yard. Do you want me to drive you over there?"

"No thanks. It's something I need to take care of myself."

"Sure thing, sweetie. You just let me know if I can help."

"Thanks Bout, I will."

Tom had showered and had begun getting dressed for his day when he heard a knock on the front door. Although he assumed the visitor was someone there to see his landlord, he peeked out his bedroom window, surprised to see Jackie's car in the driveway. After he finished buttoning his shirt, he went downstairs, opened the front door, and greeted Jackie standing on the front porch.

"Tom, I'm sorry to bother you at home, but this couldn't wait," she said, obviously embarrassed at her presence. "I need to apologize about last night."

"You already did, didn't you?" Tom answered, not yet feeling the need to relieve her of her embarrassment.

"Yeah, but I didn't think I did it well enough. And for the other thing, too. Tom, I'm so sorry. I had no idea you had heard what my friends said in the barn. I feel so embarrassed about that and for not putting a stop to it like I should have. I have no excuses, Tom, but please know how sorry I am."

Looking into Jackie's eyes, Tom could see genuine contrition. It immediately calmed his spirit.

"I've got an hour before I need to leave for class, you want to sit down for a minute?" he asked, pointing to a pair of rocking chairs on the porch.

"I'd love to."

"So how are your friends?" he asked sarcastically, obviously indifferent to their wellbeing. "And what are you doing with such a jerk? You deserve better than him."

"I'm not actually *with* him, Tom," Jackie explained. "My dad and his dad have been friends for years, and we've dated some the past couple of years, but believe me, he had much higher expectations for our relationship than did I. Don't worry, he's never taking me out again, I can assure you."

"Well, that's good to hear. I mean…it's good for you," he added, producing a smile on her face.

Jackie continued.

"Anyways, I wanted to come by and invite you to our house for supper. You know, just a way of saying I'm sorry for what happened. Plus, it'll be a way for me to get to know you better, my dad too. You've been working for us for over a year, and I feel like I barely know you. You're definitely starting to get the hang of horseback riding, although you've still got a long way to go," she said with a wry smile, while gently nudging him with her foot.

"Other than that, I know you're from Georgia; you're studying business agriculture, or some such thing, and you served in the war. Everything else about you seems to be a mystery."

"Sounds like you've been talking to Bout," Tom said with a sly smile.

"He's a good employee," she replied, her smile now beaming.

"I don't suppose you've run this by your father, have you?" asked Tom.

"Believe it or not, inviting you over was actually his idea. He always had his doubts about Lyle. Considered him too much of suck-up. When I told him about what happened last night, he called Lyle's father and told him Lyle had better not show up at our house ever again. Then he thought it'd be a good idea to have you over for supper."

"Well, I reckon I better say yes. I'm thinking my job might be on the line."

"You're right," Jackie said with a laugh, "if you say no, I'll tell my dad to fire you."

CHAPTER SIXTEEN

Well Butter My Butt and Call Me a Biscuit

From their very first meeting in the barn, when Tom startled Jackie's horse, Shadow, he felt an immediate attraction to her. While he never allowed himself to believe anything more than a friendship could ever be possible, Tom enjoyed the infrequent invitations from Jackie to join her on horseback rides around their property, sometimes stopping along a creek bank for a picnic lunch she had prepared. After the unfortunate event in the barn, when Tom overheard the conversation between Jackie and her two friends, he became doubtful even a friendship between them could exist.

As their interactions had been mostly limited to small talk, Jackie learned from Tom about where he had grown up, a little about his family, and what he had been studying at school. His involvement in the war, something Tom had been reluctant to talk about, she learned from Bout.

The *Lyle incident* at *The Front Porch*, followed by her apology and supper invitation, seemed to reestablish a friendship Tom had thought lost. He became excited about showing up for work again, hoping to spend whatever time he could with Jackie. Their friendship continued to blossom over the next few months, and Jackie became less wary of her dad discovering she had developed an attraction for one of his employees. Because of the mistaken assumption Jackie made of what her father's reaction would be, should he learn of her attraction to Tom, she did her best to hide these feelings from him. Fathers, however, can sometimes see things their children might think they don't.

Roy Duke had always been a man of high ideals, with an immenseness of character and integrity recognized by all who knew him. After his wife died giving birth to Jackie, he completely devoted himself to his work and the raising of his daughter. A successful businessman in his own right, Roy began dating a year after losing his wife. A couple of those relationships had become serious, causing many of his friends to believe he might be contemplating getting married again. But in the end, he decided against marrying, primarily because none of those women looked at him the way Jackie's mother did.

Roy Duke was also a patriot, a man who loved his country and all it stood for. Too young to serve his country in battle during the first world war, he was a single father in his early thirties when the second one broke out and felt volunteering to go fight in the war would neither be prudent nor in the best interest of his young daughter. His respect for those who did serve, however, had become immeasurable.

Having liked Tom from the beginning, Roy complemented his foreman several times on making a good hire.

"You got us a good one, Bout," he told his foreman on more than one occasion.

"Yep, he ain't half bad," Bout would always reply.

Roy appreciated the manner in which Tom conducted himself while in his employ, and the respect Tom showed whenever they spoke to one another. When Bout told him about Tom being a veteran of World War II, his respect and admiration increased exponentially. Roy once asked Tom about his service but immediately detected some reticence on Tom's part to talk about it, so he never brought the subject up again. It did not, however, diminish the esteem in which he held Tom.

While he never encouraged nor discouraged his daughter to pursue a more meaningful relationship with Tom, it became apparent to Roy his daughter's friendship with Tom had developed into something of more significance.

One day, after Tom finished his chores in the horse barn, he was invited by Roy to join Jackie and him for a glass of iced tea on the porch. As they sat and talked, Tom began telling Roy a story about his dog Amos, and their life together on their farm in Georgia. As he listened, Roy's gaze moved from Tom's face to his daughter's, sitting beside Tom on the front porch swing, staring at him as he spoke.

In this exact moment, Roy confirmed for certainty the relationship between his daughter and Tom was no longer one of mere friendship. The look he saw in his daughter's eyes he had seen only once before, and it immediately caused a stir in his heart. Jackie looked at Tom the same way her mother used to look at him, causing Roy to reach for his glass of tea, hoping to clear the sudden lump in his throat.

After Tom left, Jackie stood on the porch, waving goodbye, as Tom's truck drove down the driveway and finally out of sight. As Jackie began gathering the glasses and pitcher to take inside, Roy gently placed his hands on his daughter's shoulders, staring into her eyes.

"He's one heck-of-a good boy, Jackie," he said, his eyes conveying to his daughter the tremendous amount of unconditional love his heart was feeling at that moment.

"I know daddy. I know," she replied, setting down the half-filled pitcher of tea and embracing her father. "I was so afraid you would never approve, daddy, but I really like him, you know?"

"Of course, I know sweetie. I'm not blind. And I'm not stupid either!"

They both laughed.

"You know, your granddaddy on your mother's side had not been too keen on me at one point," Roy said.

"What are you talking about, daddy? Granddad loved you," Jackie replied, not buying it for a second.

"Well, let's just say it took a little while for me to grow on him. But you have nothing to worry about with me as far as Tom is concerned. I think he's the finest fella I've ever seen you with, and I whole-heartedly approve if you want to take this to the next level."

"I think I do, daddy, but I'm not sure how far Tom wants to go," Jackie cautiously admitted to her father.

"Well, I'm no expert," Roy replied, "but I see the way he looks at you and I'm pretty sure he thinks you hung the moon."

"Oh, daddy, give me a break. He does not," she sheepishly replied.

"I wouldn't be so sure, little darlin'. I think I can recognize when a man's been smitten."

Smiling back at her dad, grateful for his reassuring words, she felt more love for him right then than any other time she could remember.

"I hope you're right, daddy. I hope you're right."

***

Because of his increased course load, Tom was on pace to graduate by the summer of 1949. The letters he had been sending home to his mother had begun mentioning Jackie more and more, until finally they spoke of little else. Which is why Emma was not surprised when she opened a letter from Tom in the spring, announcing his intentions to marry her right after graduation.

Shortly after receiving the news of Tom and Jackie's impending marriage, Emma received a phone call from Jackie, inviting Emma to come and stay at their house for a few weeks prior to the ceremony, scheduled to take place at the Luverne Golf and Country Club.

"I'd be honored to, Jackie," Emma replied to the invitation. "I'm so looking forward to meeting you and your father."

Earl and Bobby were both now married, with Earl's wife giving birth to their first child a few months back. Bobby's wife had recently become pregnant and expected to have their first child sometime later in the year. They told their mother they would drive over for the wedding, and she should go and have a good time.

Jackie fixed a beautiful meal for them on Emma's first night in town, instantly impressing her future mother-in-law and assuaging any doubts she may have had about the well-being of her youngest son's future health. Not that any such impression would be necessary, knowing what she did about Jackie from Tom's letters. Emma had no doubt in her mind she would love Jackie the moment she laid eyes on her, and her expectations proved to be accurate.

Long after Tom returned to his house for the night and Roy excused himself to go to bed, Jackie and Emma stayed up late into the night talking and getting to know each other. The bond between them was instant, sincere and loving. When Emma looked into Jackie's eyes, she saw the face of a beloved daughter, and she couldn't have been happier Jackie would soon be a member of the family.

"Tom told me you grew up not too far from here, Mrs. Franks," Jackie said.

"First off, please call me Emma. You make me feel so old," she replied, shaking her head and smiling at Jackie. "And yes, I grew up in Montgomery, just up the road a piece. It's been so long since I've been back, I'm sure it looks nothing like it did when I was a girl. But it sure feels good to be back in Alabama, I can tell you that," she added with a smile.

"Tom told me about his dad and his brother, James," Jackie said solemnly. "I wish I could have met them."

"They would've loved you, Jackie, I can say that for sure," she replied. "Earl and Bobby will be coming over for the wedding. Earl and his wife have a beautiful little baby boy, about three months old, and Bobby and his wife are expecting their first, probably around Christmas."

"I can't wait to meet them," Jackie replied with a smile.

"So, have you and Tom talked about where you're going to live after you get married?" Emma asked with some degree of trepidation, suddenly realizing it was a subject she had never broached with Tom.

The question caught Jackie off guard a bit, since she and Tom had already decided they would live in Georgia, where he could implement some of the changes he wanted to do at their farm. Jackie had been under the mistaken assumption Tom had already discussed this with his mother, but apparently this had not been the case.

"Actually, Tom has gone on and on about things he wants to do with your farm back home. How he's got a bunch of ideas to make it real profitable. I wish I could say I knew the first thing about his degree or about farming in general, but the truth is I don't know anything about it. But I trust he knows what he's talking about. Anyways, if it's alright with you, we'd like to come live with you on your farm."

Emma's chest almost exploded, as she did a poor job of containing her excitement.

"Oh, my word Jackie, nothing would make me happier. We have so much more room now since Earl and Bobby moved out."

"To be honest, Emma, I feel a little uncomfortable telling you this," Jackie said. "I just assumed Tom had already discussed all of this with you. He told me he wants to build a big extension onto your house where we will live. Says Earl and Bobby owe him for helping them build their houses. Tom wants to start a family right away, and I'm kind of looking forward to becoming a mother myself. I can't wait to see the look in my daddy's face the first time he gets to hold his grand baby."

Emma's face now beamed. She wouldn't have cared if Jackie told her they wanted to live in a tree house on their farm. The fact her son was coming back home, and bringing with him a new daughter for Emma, made her happier than she thought possible.

"I don't think I've ever been happier in my life," Emma said, reaching out with both arms and wrapping them around Jackie. "I promise you, you're gonna love Georgia. It's almost as nice as Alabama," she added with a wink.

Emma and Jackie finally ended their discussion, deciding it was time they went to bed. Emma knew there would be little chance of her falling asleep any time soon. Floating on cloud nine, somewhere high in the heavens, nothing in the world could have brought her down.

CHAPTER SEVENTEEN

Dressed Out in Sunday-Go-To-Meetin' Clothes

<u>Luverne, Alabama, 1949:</u>

Three hundred white folding chairs, in perfect alignment, sat beneath the massive pergola adjacent to the eighteenth green at the Luverne Golf and Country Club. A canopy of sweet-smelling wisteria covered the top of the pergola, providing shade for the guests attending Tom and Jackie's wedding.

Two days before the wedding, Tom and Jackie drove to the bus station in town to pick up a very special invitee to their event… Melissa Rich and her seven-year-old son, Alex. By now, Tom had shared a great deal with Jackie about his time spent in the war, specifically stories about Richie and how he had saved his life. Jackie insisted she be invited to the wedding, even suggesting how appropriate it would be to have Alex stand up with Tom, in place of his father. Once again, Tom looked at Jackie and realized how lucky he had been to have found such an awesome woman.

Melissa could not have been more excited when she received her invitation in the mail from Jackie, which contained a personal message from her:

Outside of our own immediate families, we cannot think of anyone who would bless us more with their presence than you and your darling son. This wonderful occasion is only possible because of Richie, and I will be forever in your debt because of him. Also, we would be honored to have Alex stand with Tom during the ceremony, occupying a place of honor rightfully belonging to Richie.

The words touched Melissa in a meaningful way, and she felt an immediate bond with Jackie. A bond to remain unbroken until the end of their lives.

Tom stood beside Jackie with his arm around her back, as Melissa and Alex stepped off the bus. As soon as Alex spotted Tom, he rushed to him and jumped into his arms, shouting, "Uncle Tom, we're here!"

Jackie, unable to control the tears flowing down her cheeks, immediately embraced Melissa, whose eyes also began to moisten. After a long and heartfelt embrace, Tom made a formal introduction, which he instantly realized had been entirely unnecessary.

"I'm so happy you came, Melissa," Jackie said, as she wiped away her tears. Laughingly, she added, "Look at me, I'm blubbering like a baby!"

"Me too," Melissa replied, as Tom smiled and rolled his eyes.

"Let's get out of here," Tom said. "There's a horse this boy needs to ride, and he's waiting for us in his barn."

"Yeah!" screamed Alex with delight. "Let's go!"

***

Sharply dressed in a black tuxedo, Tom stood at the front beside the Baptist minister conducting the ceremony, anxiously waiting for Jackie to walk down the aisle on the arm of her dad. Looking handsome in a tuxedo of his own, Alex stood next to Tom holding his hand, smiling at his mother seated in the front row beside Emma. Standing beside Alex was Earl and Bobby, beaming with pride for their little brother.

Beautifully attired in a blush pink chiffon gown, a gift from her soon-to-be daughter-in-law, Emma sat with hanky in hand, blotting away tears which had already begun to flow. Accompanying Melissa and Emma in the front row were Bobby's wife Lisa and Earl's wife Katie, holding their four-month-old son, Eddie.

A large pipe organ, positioned in the grass outside the door of the clubhouse, began playing Mendelssohn's *Wedding March,* prompting all those gathered to rise from their seats, in anticipation of Jackie's grand entrance.

From Tom's vantage point, he could see all the way down the aisle, catching his first glimpse of Jackie in her wedding gown as she and her dad walked out of the clubhouse door. Gazing at the woman who would soon become his bride, his face could not hide his delight, as her father began walking her down the aisle. Earl gave Tom a quick nudge with his elbow, just in case he wasn't paying attention.

Jackie wore a beaded Venice lace trumpet-wedding gown, with a bateau neckline, its bodice bedecked with elegant embroidery. Her voluminous tulle and lace skirt with its sweep train, billowing downward from her tiny waist, whisked away the dozens of rose pedals covering the white fabric aisle runner as she sauntered in Tom's direction. Her stunning ensemble was complimented with a white flower and netted hair clip adorned to her beautifully coiffed hair. She looked more beautiful than Tom ever could have imagined. Gasps could be heard as she passed by each row and into the view of the attendees. Like Tom, many of them had never seen a more beautiful sight.

When the minister concluded the proceedings by announcing, "I now pronounce you man and wife, you may kiss the bride," Tom leaned in and kissed Jackie on the lips, as the crowd erupted in applause. Feeling almost surreal, Tom wondered how one person could ever deserve the happiness he felt in this moment.

Banquet-sized tables full of delicious food awaited the guests inside the clubhouse for the reception. A roast beef carving station anchored one of the tables, with others brimming with fresh vegetables, warm buttery rolls and a plethora of tasty, sweet desserts. Roy spared no expense in providing his only child with the wedding of her dreams.

"Look mom, it's a horse!" Dot shrieked, as she ran over to a champagne fountain with a large ice sculpture of Shadow affixed on top.

"Yes, honey," replied her mother. "It's Miss Jackie's horse, Shadow. Perhaps we'll have time to go see him before we go back home. He lives with Miss Jackie and her dad on their farm."

"I'm ready to go right now, momma," she replied excitedly.

"I know sweetheart, but you're going to have to be patient. We'll get there soon enough."

The wedding ceremony and the reception which followed were events everyone who attended would talk fondly about for years to come.

"I just wanted to make sure and send you kids off in style," Roy told Tom and Jackie, expressing their thanks for the beautiful wedding and reception he provided.

"You did a lot more than that, sir," Tom replied. "I can't tell you how much my mother has enjoyed herself. I don't remember ever seeing her this happy before."

Placing a hand on Tom's shoulder, gently squeezing him for emphasis, Roy added, "Well, she deserves to be happy, Tom. Your mother is one of the finest people I've ever met. I'm honored to know her."

After saying goodbye to Emma, Earl, Bobby and their wives, who left to head back home to Georgia, Tom and Jackie drove to the train station in Montgomery, looking forward to their weeklong honeymoon in Atlanta. Upon their return, they would load their belongings into Tom's truck and drive to Georgia to begin their new life together. Tom's first order of business would be to build a horse barn for Shadow, who Roy promised to bring over as soon as it was completed.

Roy viewed the one hundred and ninety miles soon to separate him from his daughter, as nothing more than a minor inconvenience he would gladly exchange for his daughter's happiness. He had no doubt Jackie had found the man of her dreams, and he couldn't be happier for her.

***

As soon as Tom returned home from his honeymoon, he sat down with Earl and Bobby to discuss some of the ideas he had for their farm. He flipped open a large sketchpad on the table before them, showing a drawing he made of their 200-acre plot of land. Earl and Bobby leaned in to listen to their younger brother's presentation of the changes he envisioned and his ideas of how they would be implemented.

"Right now, we're farming on about seventy acres of our land," he began, pointing to those areas marked on his sketch. "Our homes and what pastureland there is make up about twenty-five acres, leaving a little over one hundred acres of wood land. If we sell off the timber on about fifty acres, or so, and more efficiently use the seventy acres of farmland we have now, I think we can immediately double our current harvest output. The money we get from the lumber company for selling our trees, we can put right back into upgrading our farming equipment, maybe even buy a new tractor and combine."

"I'm not sure we'll get enough from the timber sales to pay for the new equipment you're talking about," Earl offered.

"Yeah, you're right, but it'll give us enough liquidity to make a loan from the bank more likely," Tom replied.

"Liquidity?" Bobby asked. "What the heck are you talking about?"

Smiling back at his brother, Tom replied, "Sorry. What I mean is, it will give us some cash on hand to make us less of a risk to the bank. Plus, I've put together a business plan to show the bank, laying out what our plans are and how we intend on paying them back. Jackie's dad is a pretty good businessman, so I want to run my plan by him first. He's coming for a visit in a few weeks, so I'll go over it with him then. If he likes the way it looks, I'll take it to our banker soon after."

Although initially hesitant about jumping on board with their little brother's ideas about changing the way they had been running the place since Eddie's passing, Earl and Bobby couldn't ignore the seriousness of Tom's approach to the family business. They loved their brother and welcomed his involvement, even though it might take a while for them to fully embrace the changes he was proposing. Emma, of course, was extremely supportive of her youngest son, which went a long way in convincing Earl and Bobby to give his ideas a chance.

"Just listen to your brother," she cautioned them. "You know he only wants what's best for all of us."

"Dang, Tommy, it looks like you actually paid attention when you were going to school over in Alabama," Earl sarcastically remarked.

"Well, I certainly didn't waste my time, if that's what you mean," Tom replied.

"I'll say," added Bobby, "you got a degree…and Jackie as a bonus. I'd say you made out pretty well."

"Agreed, but let's get back to the farm," Tom replied, trying to get his brothers refocused on the task at hand.

Flipping to the next page in his sketchpad, Tom continued with his presentation. They were now looking at a new drawing of their property, with Tom's proposed changes. Pointing to an area of trees marked with a red pencil, Tom continued.

"Once we get rid of the trees and get the stumps ground down, this area here will open up as more land for planting crops. We'll have a total of about a hundred and twenty acres we can plant on, and I've separated the area into four different quadrants."

"Whoa, now, little brother. *Quadrant*?" Bobby said with a smile.

"Knock it off Bobby, you know what I mean. Don't be a smart aleck," Tom replied, rolling his eyes at Earl who snickered at Bobby's remark.

"Each of the…*sections*…will be about thirty acres apiece," Tom continued, giving Bobby a sly look. "I propose we begin a rotation system of planting four different crops each year: tobacco, corn, soybeans and peanuts. Each section will have a separate crop, which we will rotate to a different quadrant year after year."

"I like it," Earl commented.

"Sounds good to me," Bobby added.

"Here's the last thing I'll mention," Tom said, flipping the page yet again. "With all due respect to dad, he never took full advantage of the land we used to plant each year, allowing maximum output of crops at harvest time. By adjusting the manner in which we lay out the rows for planting in each quadrant," he continued, pointing to his drawings of the four separate sections, "we can get more plants in the ground and increase the yearly yields. Anyways, this is what I've got for now. Any questions?"

"Impressive little brother," Earl remarked. "I wouldn't even know what to ask."

"Me neither," added Bobby. "I think it sounds great. I guess we'll wait to hear what your father-in-law has to say about it and then we'll go from there."

***

When Roy showed up for his visit, it had only been a little over a month since giving his daughter away, but felt much longer… not only to him, but Jackie as well. It was the longest separation the two had endured since Jackie's birth.

Emma, ever the consummate hostess, prepared an elaborate meal for Roy, with help from Jackie. As glad as she had been to see her father again, Jackie became ecstatic over being reunited with Shadow. His new living quarters, while not nearly as big or elaborate as his old, was nonetheless close in terms of comfort. He settled in quite nicely after taking Jackie for a much needed and long-awaited ride.

Following supper, Emma and Jackie cleared away the dishes and excused themselves to the kitchen, allowing Tom and Roy to spend some time alone. Tom had mentioned to Roy earlier in the day he wanted to discuss a business plan he had drawn up for the farm, and Roy happily offered to oblige him.

In a little over an hour, Tom laid out in meticulous detail every aspect of his plan, including what he anticipated to make from selling timber, how much he and his brothers would need to invest in new equipment, and how much he would need to borrow from the bank to get everything started.

Roy, thoroughly impressed by what he heard from his son-in-law, quietly rubbed his chin while flipping through the papers in front of him.

"You obviously have spent a lot of time putting this together, Tom," Roy said, "and I can't think of anything to make this plan any better. But I do have one suggestion I would like you to think about."

"Absolutely, what is it?"

"I've been in business for a long time, Tom," Roy began, "and I pride myself on being able to spot a good business opportunity when I see one. And I think I'm looking at one right now. Here's what I'm thinking: instead of going to the bank and taking out a loan, why not allow me to provide you with all the capital you'll need to put your plan into action."

"Now mind you, I'm not talking about a loan. I'm one who believes it is rarely a good idea for family members to borrow money from one another. I'm talking about allowing me to invest in your business. It won't be a loan you'll have to pay back. Instead, as your business becomes profitable, you can just pay me a portion of net profits, which will only come after paying all your expenses, including a salary for you and your brothers. To be honest with you, I wouldn't expect to see a dime for at least three or four years."

"It's unbelievably gracious of you, Roy, but I would never think of asking you for money."

"Well, as a matter of fact, you didn't," Roy replied. "I offered. And I want you to be clear about one thing, Tom. I don't view this as simply investing in a farming business. I'm investing in you,

Tom. I believe in you, and not just because you are married to my daughter, although it does help a little bit," he added with a smile.

"To be perfectly honest with you, it would be the best business investment I ever made in my life," Roy continued. "And don't forget, Tom, when I die, hopefully not anytime soon, Jackie gets everything I own, which will include my piece of your farm. Believe me, it's a win-win for both of us."

"Honestly, Roy, I'm kind of at a loss for words right now," Tom said, trying to fight off the tears he suddenly felt in his eyes. "Tell you what, I'll sit down with Earl and Bobby and see how they feel about it. Plus, I'll make sure Jackie is okay with it. Can I let you know something tomorrow?"

"Of course, Tom. You take all the time you need," Roy replied. "You must be comfortable with this or I won't. I'll respect your decision whatever it is, I'm just grateful you'll consider it."

"I'm the grateful one, Roy, believe me."

CHAPTER EIGHTEEN

Fair to Middlin'

A couple of months after Tom and his brothers had begun the construction project on their mom's home, a beautiful 2,000 sq. ft. addition where Tom and Jackie would live, completion was near. Tom knew he could never duplicate the living environs Jackie had been used to, but he wanted to make it as nice as he possibly could. Jackie couldn't care less about her new home being as plush and modern as her old; she would be happy living in a lean-to, so long as she went to bed each night beside Tom.

As Tom finished painting one of the window sashes in a spare room of their addition, Jackie brought him a glass of iced tea, while Emma quietly hid outside the door.

"What do think we'll use this room for?" she asked Tom

"Oh, I don't know. Anything, I guess. Maybe we can make it into a guest room for your dad."

"Yeah, I guess that's not a bad idea," Jackie replied, looking back at the doorway and smiling at Emma. "But my dad doesn't really need his own room. He stayed in your mom's guest room last time, and he seemed pretty comfortable there. I'm thinking maybe we could make this into a nursery."

Taking a few seconds for Jackie's last statement to sink in, Tom suddenly stopped painting and snapped his head around, looking at Jackie's face, now beaming.

"What?" he screamed, as the paintbrush in his hand bounced off the floor, splashing white paint everywhere.

He grabbed Jackie tightly with both hands on her shoulders, looking her straight in the eyes, as she continued smiling broadly, enjoying the reaction she saw in Tom's face.

"Are you serious right now?" he asked, gently shaking her back and forth as he spoke. "Tell me you're kidding."

"I'm not," Jackie replied, beginning to laugh.

"You're not what? You're not serious or you're not kidding?"

Emma couldn't stay outside any longer. She burst into the room with the biggest smile on her face she could produce.

"I'm not kidding," Jackie answered.

"You mean we're having a baby?" Tom asked, as Emma reached her arms around his neck and began hugging him.

"I think it's exactly what she means," Emma said, as Tom leaned back against the wall, a dumbfounded look covering his face.

"Jackie, why don't you go call your daddy, I'll stay here and tend to your lump-of-a husband," Emma said, smiling at Tom now seated on the floor, his eyes glazed over with a smile frozen on his face.

***

<u>Morven, Georgia, 1953:</u>

172

With the 25-foot disc harrow unit attached to the back of his tractor, Tom could plow in one day what it once took his father more than a week to plow twenty years earlier. When it came time to harvest his corn, peanut and soybean crops, his new combine could accomplish the task in one-tenth the time it took him before, allowing for a more plentiful harvest. Much of the tasks relating to the growing and harvesting of tobacco plants had remained unchanged, only now Tom and his brothers could afford to hire farmhands to do the difficult work by hand, like they had done as boys.

The investments made in new farming equipment began paying dividends in only two years, sooner than even Roy had imagined. The Franks farm was producing ten times the harvest it once did, all on account of Tom's vision and intellect. Earl and Bobby could not have been more pleased with their little brother.

As two-year-old Tom Jr. played with his trucks on the front porch, Jackie relaxed on the porch swing, as Emma came out of the door with a pitcher of cold iced tea.

"Have y'all settled on a name for this one?" Emma asked, pouring her daughter-in-law a glass of tea and handing her a wet cloth to relieve her discomfort from the sweltering heat.

"This one is going to be bigger than Tommy, I think," Jackie replied.

A little over eight months pregnant with their second child, Jackie held her large stomach like she would a beach ball and replied, "If it's a girl we want to name her after my mother, *Karen*. For a boy, Tom likes the name *James Robert,* after his brothers."

"Oh, Jackie, I think it's wonderful. Both are fine names. I just pray for a healthy baby, no matter what y'all have."

"Me too, momma. Can you believe there had actually been a time when I thought my daddy would never approve of your son?" Jackie said, laughing at herself for having such a foolish thought. "I remember the first time we met, I thought he was the most handsome man I had ever seen. I'm almost embarrassed to admit this, but the more we became friends, I started to imagine something might actually come of this. I never let on to daddy I might be having feelings for Tom, thinking he would never approve. How stupid could one person be? I think my daddy might love Tom even more than I do," she added with a laugh.

"Not so stupid, darling," Emma said with a smile. "I'm sure a lot of daddies don't think any man is good enough for their daughter. At least in the beginning."

"Is that how it was with your daddy, when you met Mr. Eddie?"

"I think so, yes, but my Eddie seemed to charm the pants off my father from the get-go. The first time we met, he had just gotten back from the war and was dressed out in his military uniform, walking down the street in a parade, right in front of my father's store. As soon as the parade ended, he high tailed it back to the store and came inside to introduce himself to my daddy and me. I think it impressed my father. Anyways, my dad invited him over for supper right then, and the rest, as they say, is history."

"That's so funny," Jackie remarked. "The first time we had Tom over for supper it was my daddy's idea, too. How long did it take for you to know Mr. Eddie was the one for you?"

"Not long, honey. Like maybe a minute or two," she said, as both laughed. "I don't know, just something about the way he made me feel. It's kind of hard to explain, but I never had a doubt about him. About a week after we met, I knew I never wanted to be with another man. Now he wasn't perfect, mind you. Lord knows we had our issues from time to time. Your father-in-law could be one stubborn man at times, I can tell you. But I never doubted for a second how much he loved me. Nothing in life is perfect, sweetie, but my Eddie made me feel like I was the most special person who ever lived. He was a gift from God, and he gave me a little piece of heaven right here on earth."

"Well, I can't honestly say I felt the same about Tom quite as quickly as you, but I do know what you mean," Jackie said. "When I look at Tom, Earl and Bobby, and when I hear stories about James, I'm amazed at how good a momma you were to them. How well they were raised, I mean, just look at how good they all turned out. I know I could never be as good a mother as you were, but I want to try. Sometimes I worry about failing them. Do you know what I mean?"

"Don't be ridiculous. You're already a better mother than me," Emma replied, reassuring Jackie. "You wouldn't say as much if you knew half the mistakes I made."

"Oh, c'mon now, like what? You seem absolutely perfect to me."

"Not hardly, sweetheart. Ask Bobby sometime about the time he came in the house complaining about his arm hurting after falling out of that very tree over there," Emma said, pointing to a large White Oak about twenty yards from where they sat.

"I was inside fixing supper, and I told him to turn right back around and go back outside, and not to come back in until I called him," Emma continued. "He must've been about seven or eight years old at the time. Anyways, he woke up the next morning still complaining about his arm hurting. Even then, I didn't do anything about it. Just told him to try not to use it and it would feel better soon enough. How's that for good motherly advice? The next day, which was two days after he fell mind you, he couldn't even lift his arm. Eddie drove him to town to have the doctor look at it, and lo and behold, it was broken in two places. Now how bad do you think I felt after that?"

"Oh, my goodness momma, I guess you're not perfect after all," Jackie laughingly said.

"A long way from it, darling. But I will tell you this, and it's the same advice my mother gave to me," Emma said, turning more serious. "You can't protect your kids from everything in this world, 'cause it's impossible to be by their side all the time, especially as they get older. You've got to pray for them, dear. And I don't mean just every now and then. I'm talking about every day, multiple times a day, every time the thought crosses your mind."

"So, you prayed for them a lot?"

"Honey, I got nothing but bone left in the tops of my knees," Emma said, tapping one of her knees with her hand. "All the padding is gone, wore out a long time ago from all the time I spent kneeling beside my bed. Being a mother is the best job in the history of mankind, and probably the hardest. If you think you can do it on your own, you're being foolish. The Good Lord is there to help us whenever we ask, so don't ignore Him. Believe me, you won't regret it."

"That might be the best advice I've ever heard, momma. I think I'll take back what I said a minute ago."

"What's that?"

"When I said you're NOT perfect," Jackie replied, smiling at Emma who had unquestionably become the mother she never had…and the mother she longed to be.

***

Three and a half years after the birth of James, Karen made her grand entrance into the world, completing Tom and Jackie's family. While Tom equally loved all three of his children, the feeling he had when he looked into the face of his precious daughter was something he had never experienced before. There's something special about a father-daughter relationship which is a little different than with sons, and Tom felt it the day they brought Karen home from the hospital. Imbued with the same protective instincts inherited from his father, six-year-old Tom Jr. made it his life's mission to be her ultimate protector. Jimmy, who tried to do everything his older brother did, would soon feel the same way.

Jackie's father Roy, now semi-retired, left the day-to-day running of *Duke Family Horse Farm* in the capable hands of Robin Boutwell, his trusted and dedicated employee for nearly twenty years. He wore out the highway between his home in Luverne, Alabama, and Morven, Georgia, where his daughter and her family lived. Besides longing to see Jackie and his three grandchildren, Roy loved spending time with Emma, a person he had come to love and respect like no other, save for his own dearly departed wife.

While the bond between them had become deep and loving, neither considered their relationship more than a special friendship, both acknowledging to one another they had met and married their one true love, and there would not be another for either of them. Although Jackie often wondered aloud to Tom if there might be something *brewing* between their parents, Roy and Emma assured them one night over supper no such scenario was in the works nor ever would be. Getting it out in the open had a calming effect on all those involved and made the bond of friendship between Roy and Emma even stronger.

Roy never missed an opportunity to hop on one of Tom's tractors and take a ride around the farm, always asking Tom for permission before doing so.

"You own part of it, Roy," Tom told him. "You can take her out any time you please."

After five straight years of profits, each year surpassing the previous, the Franks farm was running like a well-oiled machine.

"I never had a doubt," Roy said to Tom, while touring the property with Tom in the cab of their newest John Deere. "Like I told you a while back, I know a good investment when I see one. I'm very proud of what you and your brothers have been able to accomplish here. But most of all, I'm grateful for the life you've provided Jackie. I sleep well at night knowing when I'm no longer around; she'll be well taken care of."

"Well, let's not get ahead of ourselves," Tom replied. "We're planning on you being around for several more years."

"I know, and so am I, by the way," Roy said with a smile. "But

I have begun thinking about what's going to happen when the Lord finally does call me home. Obviously, everything I have will go to Jackie, but she's going to need you to help her make decisions about how to handle the assets I leave behind."

Tom's face seemed to show signs of discomfort as Roy spoke, and Roy took notice.

"There really is no need for this conversation to be uncomfortable, Tom. We really do need to have it."

"I know it, I guess. It just seems a little premature."

"Now you know better than that, Tom. You're one of the smartest people I've ever known and being prepared for something we both know is going to happen one day is not being premature."

"Yeah, you're right. I'm just saying we're not going to have to worry about any of this for a long, long time."

"Well, obviously I hope you're right, Tom. I'm not anxious to go anywhere, anytime soon," Roy added with a smile.

"What about your farm?" Tom asked, turning to a serious tone while engaging his father-in-law in the conversation he knew he sought.

"It'll be for you and Jackie to decide, Tom. This is Jackie's home now, and obviously it's been yours since you were born. Y'all could keep the place in Alabama if you like, but I don't really see the sense in it, unless for some reason y'all decided to move there. But I can't see that as being a possibility. You need to stay near your mom, and I don't think you could drag her away from here if you hooked her up to the back of this big tractor," Roy said with a laugh.

"You're so right," Tom confirmed.

"There's this young guy in town, a member of the club, who I know would be interested in buying my place. He's been after me for the past few years, wanting me to sell it to him. Says he'll pay whatever I ask. Anyways, I told him thanks but no thanks. I'm just not interested. At least not right now. I don't need the money, and I don't want to live anywhere else. I'll leave you his name and number and you just keep it handy for when the time comes. But like I said, hopefully not for a while."

"Not for a LONG while," Tom added.

CHAPTER NINETEEN

Livin' In High Cotton

In 1896, the United States Supreme Court heard a case known as *Plessy v. Ferguson,* which upheld racial segregation laws for public facilities under the doctrine of *separate but equal.* The state of Louisiana, under a law passed by its legislature called the *Separate Car Act,* required separate accommodation for blacks and whites on railroads, including separate railway cars.

A group opposed to this law persuaded Homer Plessy, a black man, to participate in an orchestrated *test case* of this law. Mr. Plessy bought a train ticket for the *whites only* section on the train, took his seat, and refused to move to the *black* section when confronted by train officials. This defiance led to his arrest and the subsequent Supreme Court decision, which followed. Ruling against Mr. Plessy, the decision codified the rights of individual states to segregate people based on race, as long as *equal* public facilities existed for both blacks and whites.

Hailing from Georgia and Alabama respectively, both Tom and Jackie grew up under the stain of *Jim Crow* laws in the South, both attending segregated schools as children. Tom, especially, had many childhood friends who were black, and now employed several on his farm. The fact he and Jackie sat in school classrooms where no other children of color were present, always seemed to them to be "just the way it was."

Neither could understand the prevalent feelings amongst many they knew of the superiority of their race over another. There had never been an iota of animus in either of their hearts toward another person, based solely on the color of their skin. But for children growing up in the South in the 1930s, 1940s and 1950s, this, unfortunately, had simply been a way of life for them.

In 1954, fifty-eight years after the *Plessy* decision, the country made a sharp U-turn on the road to institutional racism it had been travelling on for decades. In *Brown v. The Board of Education of Topeka, Kansas,* a landmark decision by the U.S. Supreme Court reversing *Plessy,* the Court unanimously declared unconstitutional any state law establishing separate public schools for blacks and whites. While the decision became a major victory for proponents of the *Civil Rights Movement,* paving the way for the integration of schools and other public facilities, the decision did not spell out the manner in which such integration would take place. It only said, "*States are to desegregate with all deliberate speed,*" and suggested no time frame for this to occur.

Consequently, Tom Jr., Jim and Karen grew up attending school as their parents did, sharing their classrooms with only white children. Whenever Jackie escorted her children and a group of their friends…some who were black…into town to treat them to ice cream and candy at the local drug store, she inevitably received looks of condemnation from a few of her neighbors. Some, undoubtedly, avoided showing Jackie their disdain, primarily because of who her mother-in-law was. Tom and Jackie may have been respected in town, but Emma was feared.

Once, when a local merchant refused service to Jackie and Emma, who stood at the check-out counter with a handful of licorice sticks for the black and white children they had brought to town, Emma reacted by throwing the treats on the ground in front of the merchant. She then picked up the canister containing the remaining supply of the store's licorice sticks and dumped those on the ground as well.

"Try selling these now," she angrily told the merchant. "Let's go, Jackie. This place obviously never wants another dime from us."

As they walked from the store, Emma began to calm and quietly said to Jackie, "I probably could've handled that better."

"I think the good Lord will give you a pass on that one, momma. Like you've told me a thousand times, we're called to forgive them," replied Jackie.

"Why can't these people see every one of us is a child of God, not one better than the other," said Emma. "They may not know it, but one day they'll meet their Maker and find out how wrong they were for all these years. All you can do is raise your kids right, teach 'em the Bible, and make sure they know the difference between right and wrong. If you've done all those things, Jackie, then you've done your job. Let the Good Lord worry about the rest."

Jackie loved Emma and never went to bed at night without thanking God for allowing her time in Emma's circle. *As usual,* Jackie thought, *you're right as rain.*

***

<u>South Georgia, 1960s:</u>

Twelve-year-old Tom Jr., ten-year-old Jimmy and seven-year-old Karen were happy, respectful children, living their life in Morven, Georgia, not altogether unlike their father's, who had never known another home. The house Tom had grown up in, including the room where Emma had delivered him, no longer stood, replaced by a beautiful 5,000 sq. ft. brick Southern Plantation home. When Tom discussed with Jackie his ideas of what home to build, he offered to build her an Antebellum home, much like the one in *Gone with The Wind,* a favorite movie of hers.

"Oh Lord, Tom, have you lost your mind?" she responded to his suggestion. "You think I want people around here thinkin' I'm rich or something?"

"But you are, sweetie."

"Well, I'll be danged if I'm gonna let anyone know it!"

Emma had also been consulted and had only one requirement before assenting to the destruction of the home she had known for nearly half a century.

"I want a porch on one side of the house where I can watch the sun come up while I have my morning coffee; and one on the other side so I can see it go down and watch my grand babies play in the yard while I rock in my chair and pet Bentley."

Bentley was Tom Jr.'s seventy-pound Yellow Lab, a gift from his father on his tenth birthday. Like Amos before him, Bentley learned quickly nestling up to Emma would almost certainly result in the *accidental* dropping of a piece of bacon or some such treat, although with much less furtive movement than she had shown with Amos.

Their new home, equipped with all modern conveniences imaginable, had a massive kitchen with a 6-burner gas stove and a double-oven, things Emma could not even have imagined years earlier.

"I had an old box stove which sat under the kitchen window with a stovepipe stuck through the wall. I'd fill it with wood every morning and every evening, throw in some crumpled up newspaper, light it with a match, and use the heat from the fire to cook with. Now, all you do is flick a 'dad-blame' switch and you can cook all night long if you want to. I swanee."

Jackie couldn't stop smiling, even if she wanted to, as she listened to her mother-in-law talk about the *good ol' days* and how things used to be. Fact is, if Emma had the strength to talk on for two straight days, nonstop, about raising her family in the old house, and what their life had been like back then, Jackie would've listened to every word and longed for more when she stopped. She literally worshipped the ground Emma walked on.

"You know Jackie," Emma continued, "I used to have to heat up a kettle of water and scoop it out to give my boys a bath. Always on Saturday night, mind you, so they'd smell good for church in the morning. Who would've ever thought, nowadays you can turn a handle and take a hot shower every night if you want to. Lord, what is this world comin' to?"

Jackie didn't know how many more days God had in store for Emma to be on this earth; she just prayed she never had to miss a single one of them.

***

Cities and towns throughout the South were becoming hotbeds of civil rights related to activities in the early 1960s. Albany,

Georgia, with a population of 55,000, many of whom were black, sat sixty miles to the north of Morven. Sexual assaults by white men against black women students at Albany State College went virtually ignored by the local police, causing unrest in many of the black precincts of Albany. Local pastors and other leaders of the black community began staging protests and *sit-ins* at local *All White* lunch counters, as a way of bringing attention to the plights of the black community there.

The Albany Movement, a desegregation coalition formed in November of 1961, had been the driving force behind many of these protests. Prior to its formation, voter registration, petitions and other types of civil rights-related activity had been going on for years in Albany, without much success in changing conditions for its black citizens.

One morning, as Jackie and Emma enjoyed their coffee outside on the porch, Jackie opened the latest edition of *The Valdosta Daily Times.* Many of the headlines dealt with the civil unrest going on in the country, not just around them, but also throughout the South.

"Every time I read one of these stories, momma, it makes me die a little inside," Jackie commented. "How can so many people be so wrong about something? Tom thinks it's going to get a lot worse before it gets better. I'm starting to think he may be right."

"I know, darling," Emma replied. "It makes me sad to think about how little progress has been made around here since I first moved here. Did I ever tell you the story of one of those *Klansmen* coming here to try and talk my Eddie into joining up with them?"

"Yes," Jackie replied with a smile. "It's just a shame we don't have more men like him around here."

Jackie continued perusing the front page of her paper when an article caught her attention.

"Hey momma, listen to this," Jackie said, looking down at her paper. "There's a big meeting planned for tomorrow up in Albany. A young preacher from Atlanta is coming to speak. Somebody named Martin Luther King, Jr. Says he used to be the pastor of Dexter Avenue Baptist Church in downtown Montgomery. Isn't that where your daddy had his store?"

"Sure is. I used to play on the steps of that church. It was only about two blocks from daddy's shop. What else does it say about this preacher?"

"Says he led the Montgomery Bus Boycott a few years ago and has been thrown in jail a few times for trying to incite civil unrest," Jackie replied, as she read some of the article out loud to Emma. "I guess when someone says you can't drink out of a water fountain, or sit down in a restaurant like everyone else, you're supposed to shut up and obey. I swear, some of these people really make me sick!"

"You wanna go?" Emma asked Jackie, with a sudden look of excitement on her face.

"Are you serious? I'd love to go. I think I'd like to meet this preacher."

It took Tom a minute or two to warm up to the idea, but eventually consented when he saw how much attending the meeting in Albany meant to his wife and mother.

"As long as I can go with you," he said. "Some of these things have a way of getting out of hand, and I want to be there in case it does."

"We'd love for you to go with us," Jackie said, excited for the chance to go hear Reverend King and possibly meet him.

A few weeks prior to Rev. King's arrival, members of *The Albany Movement* staged several non-violent protests throughout the city, including an attempt to end segregation at the Albany Bus Depot, in accordance with recently passed federal regulations mandating bus depots serving interstate passengers may not be segregated. The local police chief, aware of the impending efforts of the coalition, had his officers on site, ready to make arrests for *disturbing the peace*. The episode remained essentially non-violent, resulting in the coalition accomplishing little.

At the same time, other black activists attempted to occupy areas in libraries and lunch counters reserved for *whites only*, as well as march on City Hall, all in protest of the disparate treatment blacks were receiving. In all of these instances, the police chief had devised a plan to counter the protests, ordering his officers to make non-violent arrests, imploring them to avoid any violence which may bring undue attention and sympathy to the protestors. His tactics were generally successful, as the day of protest by *The Albany Movement* had minimal effect.

Rev. King's visit would be his attempt to prop up the movement, not wanting to see the mood of the protestors abated. His address, which took place at the Shiloh Baptist Church in Albany, was well attended and included the presence of Tom, Jackie and Emma. Following his speech, Rev. King stood on the front steps of the church, greeting many of those who attended. As Tom, Jackie and Emma were but a very few of those white who attended, the reverend spent a little extra time shaking hands and speaking with them, expressing his gratitude for their support.

"Thank you for stopping by," Rev. King remarked. "Where are y'all from?"

"Morven, Reverend King, about an hour south of here," Tom answered.

"Ah yes, I know it well. Beautiful little town," the reverend replied.

Tom didn't know if he was being totally honest or just being nice. Regardless, his wife and mother were euphoric over the remark and couldn't stop talking about their encounter with Rev. King all the way home.

"What a nice young man," Emma said. "He seemed so pleasant."

"Yes, and boy can he speak!" Jackie added.

Much to their chagrin, Emma and Jackie opened the following morning's paper, only to learn Rev. King and a few other peaceful protestors had been arrested, only hours after their encounter on the steps of Shiloh Baptist Church.

"How awful," Jackie remarked. "To think of that poor man having to spend time in jail for trying to get the same rights for his people the rest of us already have. It's pathetic. What's wrong with these people?"

Unfortunately, they would have to read more about the travails of Rev. King over the next few years, including his arrest and abuse at the hands of the Birmingham police in Jackie and Emma's home state of Alabama.

"Makes me ashamed to be from there, momma," Jackie said. "What has happened to our people? Why are they so bad?"

"Same thing that's happening everywhere else," Emma answered. "This world is full of people ain't got walkin' around sense, I tell you. And it's not as simple as these people just being bad, which they are. It's a case of them being spiritually dead as well. God is the only one can change a man's heart, Jackie, and Lord help us all if these people don't soon realize it."

Unfortunately, the animosity towards people of color by their fellow Alabamians would go on for way too long, as change in attitudes toward black Americans moved along at a snail's pace.

Alabama's popular governor, George C. Wallace, whose inaugural speech included the infamous line, "segregation now, segregation tomorrow, segregation forever," defied federal law mandating the integration of public universities. His *Stand in The Schoolhouse Door* tactic was a symbolic attempt to fulfill his campaign promise to fight racial integration at every turn.

After the Alabama National Guard troops were federalized by President Kennedy, taking them out from under the authority of the Alabama governor, Governor Wallace was forced to stand aside and allow two black students the opportunity to register for classes at the University of Alabama.

Emma and Jackie wondered if, in their lifetimes, they would ever see the South they loved undergo a heart transplant and see all of their fellow citizens as they did: God's children, who are no better or no worse than them.

CHAPTER TWENTY

There's a Storm a Brewin'

The temperature had reached nearly a hundred degrees in the shade when Tom decided to break for lunch, having spent the last few hours teaching Tom Jr. how to drive the tractor.

"You ready to go inside and grab something to eat?" he asked his son.

"I'm dying, dad," Tom Jr. replied. "I'm ready to get inside where we got air conditioning. Is it true when you were a boy and lived here with Grandma Emma and Papa, y'all didn't have air conditioning?"

"You're right, son. We didn't even have a fan to keep us cool. If me and my brothers wanted to cool off, we'd just jump in the river."

"Man, it's unbelievable, dad. I don't know how you survived without air conditioning."

"It was easy for us to survive not having air conditioning, son, 'cause when I was a boy none of us knew what it was. Nobody had air conditioning, at least not around here."

"Well, I sure know what it is, and I'm glad we got it," Tom Jr. said, as he and his dad removed their boots and left them on the porch before going inside.

Walking inside the house, Tom instantly felt a temperature change of at least thirty degrees, as the blast of cool air inside hit him in the face.

"Goodness, Jackie. What you got the thermostat set on?" Tom asked, as he walked into the kitchen where Jackie had been preparing lunch. "It's colder in here than a well-digger's ass!"

Spinning around with a look of surprise on her face, Jackie couldn't believe what she just heard.

"Hush!" she whispered with some consternation, as Tom tried not to laugh at her reaction. "I don't want the kids hearing you talk like that."

Emma covered her mouth so her grandkids wouldn't hear her snicker, as Jimmy hopped up on a bar stool at the kitchen counter, gleeful as he proclaimed, "Ummm…dad said *ass*. Tommy, did you hear Dad? He said *ass*."

The look on Jackie's face could have stopped a bear in its track.

"And you're no help, momma," she said to Emma, who could no longer keep her laughter to herself.

"I'm sorry, mom," Tom said, hoping his feeble attempt at contrition would help the situation. "Boys," he continued, looking at Tom Jr. and Jimmy, while trying not to smile, "I shouldn't have said that. Don't repeat it. Okay?"

"You heard your father, boys," Jackie jumped in. "I better not hear that kinda language from either of you boys. I'll tan your hide so bad you won't sit for a week. Do you understand?"

"Yes, mom," the boys said in unison, only to burst out in laughter when their five-year-old sister walked into the kitchen, chanting "ass…ass."

Tom didn't have the guts to even look in the direction of his wife, fearing the repercussions sure to follow. He did, however, have the capacity not to smile, which probably saved him a night on the couch.

***

After supper, Jackie and Emma sat on the porch enjoying another beautiful sunset, as Tom came out to join them after cleaning up the dishes, his voluntary act of penance for his earlier behavior. Knowing he still treaded on thin ice, he brought Jackie a cup of fresh-brewed coffee and handed it to her before sitting down.

Taking advantage of an opportunity she felt had properly ripened, Jackie turned her attention to Tom.

"Momma and I have been talking about something, and we have a favor to ask."

"Sure, what is it?"

"You know about all the nonsense going on with Rev. King, right?"

"Yeah, of course."

"Well, I saw in the paper this morning he is planning a big rally in Washington, D.C. in a couple of weeks. He's calling it a *March on Washington.* Momma and I think it would be a great idea for all of us to go, the kids included. They've never been to our nation's capital and there are so many things there for them to see. Plus, I think it'd be a good idea for them to take part in the march. I want them to know which side of this issue we're on and seeing Rev. King give his speech would have a great impact on them."

Tom sat silent for a moment, looking back and forth between Jackie and Emma, before responding.

"Momma, is this your idea?" he asked Emma.

"Hey, don't blame me," Emma replied. "This is Jackie's idea, and I think it's a good one. Me and her are going. We're just being polite and asking you if you want to join us."

Tom smiled at his mother's statement, as he turned his attention back to Jackie.

"I think it's a good idea, too," he replied, knowing such a response would instantly put himself squarely back in the good graces of his wife. "Let's drive up a few days early and we can do some sightseeing along the way. Sound good to y'all?"

Jackie, a little stunned by his quick compliance, became elated.

"See, darlin'," Emma said. "I told you, you had nothing to worry about."

"Thank you so much, Tom," Jackie said, as she got up from her chair to hug him and kiss him on the cheek.

As she leaned over to put her arms around his neck, Tom reached up with one hand and gently slapped Jackie on her behind, while pulling her closer in, aggressively kissing her on her neck and face.

"Tom, stop it! the kids will see."

All three children had been playing in the yard and immediately ran up on the porch when they saw their dad *assaulting* their mother.

"Daddy spanked mommy…daddy spanked mommy," Jimmy sang, to the delight of Tom Jr. and Karen.

This time, Jackie joined in the laughter, smacking Tom on top of the head as she backed away.

"You're incorrigible Tom Franks," she said, still beaming. "Momma, I blame you. He's your boy."

"Not hardly, sweet pea," Emma remarked with a laugh. "I got shed of that boy a long time ago. He's your responsibility now."

***

On August 28, 1963, Tom and his entire family stood alongside the Tidal Basin on the Washington, D.C. Mall, and heard Martin Luther King, Jr. deliver his *I Have a Dream* speech. Amongst 250,000 other supporters, the experience forever changed the lives of Tom, Jackie and Emma, and perhaps more importantly, the lives of their three children. Emma and Jackie, emotionally impacted by the event like even they could not have imagined, vowed to start making a difference in the lives of those around them.

"We can't help everyone, Jackie, but we can sure help some," said Emma.

If they wanted to make a difference, they needed to start in their own community. As soon as they got back home to Morven,

Georgia, they began holding barbecue picnics at *Campground,* inviting anyone and everyone they could. With their goal being racial reconciliation, Jackie and Emma knew there were many in their community who would never come around to their way of thinking, but some would, and they believed in the nobility of the effort.

As they walked through the predominantly black residential areas of Morven, knocking on doors and handing out fliers of invitation to their *community picnic,* Jackie and Emma let them know they were a valuable part of the community. They also began regular visits to tutor young black children, teaching many to read and providing them with the scholarly instruction woefully lacking in their dilapidated and understaffed schools.

Over time, word spread of their involvement within the black community. Many of their white neighbors were none too pleased to see the deference being paid to black people by the Franks family, including the number of African Americans employed by Tom and his brothers to work their farm. Most of the other residents simply showed their disdain with arrogant looks and the occasionally intemperate remark. Others, however, felt it was their duty to express their displeasure in more impactful ways.

"Seems like you and your brothers are hiring a lot of coloreds to pick your tobacco, Tom," said one man who approached Tom at a local diner one afternoon. "There's a lot of white men in town who could use a paycheck."

"Well, if you got someone who can outwork the help I got, then by all means have them come by and apply for a job. We're always lookin' for good workers. In the meantime, we're gonna hire folk who are willing to put in a good day's work for a good day's pay, and that's exactly what we got."

The man, probably a local Klansman, scoffed at Tom as he turned and walked out of the diner. Perhaps the man did not know Tom owed his life to a black man, and because of that, felt a special kinship with them. More likely, this knowledge would've made absolutely no difference to the man's way of thinking.

Several weeks later, Emma and Jackie were finishing their lessons with a group of black children as dusk arrived.

"Miss Emma, you and Miss Jackie ought to finish up and get on your way," said one of the mothers. "Y'all don't need to be driving home after dark, what with how some of these town folks must think of y'all for all the kindness you been showin' us."

"She's probably right, momma," Jackie said to Emma. "Tom's told me a thousand times don't be driving home after dark."

Emma nodded in agreement as she gathered her books together and readied to leave.

As Jackie slowed her car to cross some railroad tracks on the outskirts of the "black" part of town, a set of headlights appeared in Jackie's rearview mirror. Not wanting to alarm Emma, Jackie said nothing and continued to drive, constantly looking in her mirror, praying the vehicle following her would soon turn off. When it didn't, Jackie slowed her car, hoping the vehicle behind her would simply go around. Instead, the vehicle, a pickup truck with several white men, all of whom were drunk, pulled alongside Jackie's car and began taunting them.

"Don't say a word, Jackie and just keep your eyes forward," Emma implored. "Those heathens don't have the sense God gave a goose."

A moment later, the truck sped up and passed Jackie's car, bringing them instant relief. It was short-lived, however, as the truck moved in front of her car and began to slow, weaving from side to side so as not to allow Jackie's car to pass. Finally, the truck came to a complete stop, forcing Jackie to stop as well so as not to crash into the back of them. Two of the men immediately jumped out and began walking back towards Jackie's car, as the ladies sat still, obviously in fear for their safety.

"Dear God, get us outta this mess," Emma prayed aloud.

"Well, if it ain't those nigger-lovin' white women," one of the men said as he approached the driver's side window.

"Y'all need to go on and leave us be," Emma boldly shouted as she and Jackie quickly rolled up their windows and locked their doors, trying to conceal their obvious sense of despair.

"Nah, I don't think we'll be doin' that," the man replied.

Emma had a reputation around town of being one tough cookie, but a handful of drunk men against two women on a deserted dirt road at night were not good odds. As one man began pounding on the hood of Jackie's car, the other reached for the door handle of the driver's side door, now locked. Before the men could do anything else, namely break out a window to extract Jackie and Emma from the car, a set of headlights appeared on the road ahead. Seconds later, the flashing lights of a police patrol car began rotating on top of the car, lighting up the pine trees that lined the road where they sat.

"Let's get outta here," one man said to the other, as they both ran to their truck, jumped inside, and sped off.

"Thank you, Jesus," Emma sighed, as she and Jackie unlocked their doors and got out of their car to meet the patrol car approaching.

"Everything alright, ladies?" asked the Brooks County Deputy Sheriff, as he approached Jackie and Emma.

"No deputy, it's not," stated Jackie emphatically. "That truck driving away forced us off the road and threatened to harm us. That is, until you drove up. You need to go after them. We'll be more than happy to file charges against them."

"Well, I don't think that'll be necessary. Anyways, it looks like they plum got away as it is. I don't reckon they'll be giving you anymore trouble tonight."

The deputy sheriff tipped his cap to Jackie and Emma and turned away, slowly making his way back to his patrol car. Jackie began to shout back at the deputy, but Emma cut her off before she could say anything.

"Don't waste your breath, darling. He's one of them."

Emma could not have been more right. The deputy, sympathetic to the cause of the white racists, was not about to go after one of his own. Fortunately for Jackie and Emma, he just happened along when they were forced off the road, and believing an accident had occurred ahead, turned on his police lights, which scared the racists away. Had he known what was actually transpiring, he probably would've turned around and gone back from where he came, leaving the ladies at the mercy of the men.

"The Lord was watchin' out for us, dear," Emma said as they drove away.

Tom had to let it lie. Complaining to the authorities about the deputy or the men in the truck would be a waste of time, he reasoned.

"We all just have to be more careful," he cautioned his family.

Months later, the troubles came to an awful head, as Tom, Earl and Bobby stood helplessly by, late one night, as they watched one their tobacco barns go up in flames. The blaze, no doubt the work of some local Klansmen, was meant as a message to the Franks family that their acceptance of those of another color was not to be tolerated.

Tom, Jackie and Emma would not be deterred. They continued to reach out to their brothers and sisters in the black community, and over time helped change the minds of many. The picnics continued, as more and more people realized little harm could come from all of them getting together as a community for lunch, especially when it was being provided by the Franks family.

As the event drew more people, several of the ladies began preparing their own special dishes for the occasion, turning it into a pot-luck affair. When it outgrew the available space at *Campground,* they moved next door to a large open field next to Mr. Lawson's peach orchard.

Dozens of children, black, white and brown, played together, while their parents and grandparents shared meals together, building new, lasting friendships. Jackie even brought *Rebel,* an offspring of Shadow who had passed away years earlier, so some of the kids could enjoy their first-ever horse ride.

Jackie and Emma had no desire to make a political statement, they just wanted to show their black and brown neighbors they valued them, which had been a stark departure from so many of the headlines they were reading in the *Daily Times.*

Over the years, their reading and tutoring program helped many disadvantaged young black children improve their chances of completing their education, many of whom went on to graduate from high school, who otherwise would have had little chance at doing so. Their involvement made a long-lasting difference in the lives of many in their community, all of it inspired by the impact of their encounter with Rev. King.

They both cried when they saw images coming from their television set of black protestors being beaten by Alabama police officers on the Edmund Pettis bridge in Selma, or police dogs attacking black protestors in Birmingham. At times, they felt their efforts were futile, as they continued to witness acts of racism and bigotry so prevalent in the South back then. But they pressed on.

"One at a time, Jackie," Emma said on many occasions. "It's all we can do."

***

While it came as no surprise, they were crestfallen to find out Lester Maddox had won the governorship of Georgia in 1966. Maddox had been a restaurant owner in Atlanta before he decided to seek public office. Known for its simple, inexpensive Southern cuisine, *The Pickrick* restaurant opened in 1947 next to the campus of Georgia Tech University.

A segregationist through and through, Maddox ran his restaurant as a *whites only* establishment. When the *Civil Rights Act of 1964* was passed by Congress, making it unlawful to deny access to blacks, Maddox refused to change his *whites only* policy. He filed a federal lawsuit to continue his segregationist policy, only to lose in the courts. When three black Georgia Tech students asked to be seated in the restaurant, Maddox stood in the doorway with an axe handle, threatening them with bodily harm if they tried to enter. After all possible remedies for his restaurant to remain segregated were exhausted, he decided to close it in 1965 rather than to serve black customers. And this man had just been elected governor.

"I don't know what Bible they're reading, Jackie, but it ain't the same one as mine," Emma said, disheartened over seeing how little race relations in the South had improved.

"One day, momma, one day," Jackie said, trying to encourage Emma. "Change never comes easy. We've both known as much for a while, now. All we can do is what we can do, momma. After that, the only thing left is praying for God to take care of the rest. I got that from you, you know."

"Such a sweet child," Emma said, smiling at her daughter-in-law as she squeezed her hand.

While Tom's sentiments were aligned with those of his wife's and mother's, he had a business to run. He encouraged them in their pursuit of social change, but felt his primary duty lay with the running of his farm. In 1964, while Jackie and Emma dealt with the storm of racism and bigotry, he had a storm of his own to deal with.

T.V. news reports were warning residents of south Florida of an impending hurricane bearing down on Miami, after wreaking havoc on some of the islands in the Caribbean. Without the meteorological technology available to weather forecasters of today, weathermen could only make vague predictions of where they thought a storm would head after making landfall. Some predicted the storm would move north along the eastern shoreline of Florida, and possibly impact parts of southern Georgia, before finally petering out.

Hurricane Cleo had become a massive storm, they said, producing wind and rain capable of substantially damaging anything and everything in its path. Figuring he had maybe two or three days of lead time, he went about the task of harvesting as much of his crops as possible, getting them put up and out of harm's way should *Cleo* decide to make an unwelcome visit.

Three days later, the storm made landfall just south of Savannah, Georgia, about two hundred miles northeast of his farm. While he avoided the devastating winds of the hurricane, he couldn't avoid the torrential downfall of rain it produced. What crops remained in the ground were ruined, unable to withstand the six months' worth of rainfall which fell in two days. Tom's quick action averted what could have been a disaster, providing more evidence of why he had enjoyed so much success.

CHAPTER TWENTY-ONE

Gooder than Grits

Jackie beamed with pride as she adjusted the fit of Tom Jr.'s high school graduation gown, making sure the hemline was the right length and the fit on his massive shoulders was not too tight.

"My oh my," Grandma Emma proclaimed as she looked on, "what a handsome young man you have become. I'm so proud of you."

"Thanks grandma," he replied, seemingly agitated at his mother for all the pulling and pinching.

"It's fine, mom," he pleaded. "Just leave it alone."

"I just want to make sure you look your best, son."

"Can I go now?" he asked, anxious to join his friends who were planning a night on the town to celebrate their impending freedom, less than a month away.

Tom Jr. had been accepted to attend Georgia Tech in the fall, telling his father he wanted to become an engineer.

"I don't want to be a farmer, dad," he told Tom Sr., concerned his declaration might disappoint his father. "I want to build things."

"Tommy, farming is my life. It's all I've ever done and all I know," Tom told his son. "It doesn't mean it has to be your life.

You're a man now and you need to make decisions that are best for you. Same as what I did when I was about your age. Don't you ever think for a second I'm upset about you choosing a path which doesn't include farming. If you want to be an engineer, then you go and be the best danged engineer you can possibly be. I'm confident you will make your mother and me proud, just like you always have."

"Thanks, dad, it means a lot."

As Tom Jr. bolted out the door, Jackie grabbed her purse and car keys and headed out the door with Emma. Since their meeting with Martin Luther King on the steps of Shiloh Baptist church in Albany, Emma and Rev. King had corresponded back and forth by mail several times in the ensuing years. She telling him about the things she and Jackie were doing in their community to promote better race relations; and he, updating her on some of the battles they were winning in his movement's pursuit of racial equality. His latest letter to Emma indicated he would be in Valdosta helping black city workers in their battle with city leaders over pay disparity and would like to see them to say *hello*.

***

Standing inside the room at Valdosta City Hall, Jackie and Emma listened intently as Rev. King finished speaking. As he stepped from the stage to the sound of thunderous applause, the reverend spotted the ladies and made a beeline in their direction.

"I can't believe how long it's been since our first meeting," Rev. King remarked, as Emma and Jackie swooned with excitement. "Thank you for your letters, Emma. You have no idea how much they inspire me. We're going to win this fight because of people like you. It won't happen as soon as many of us would like, but it's going to happen."

The reverend was being politely pushed along by one of his associates as he concluded his short conversation with Emma and Jackie.

"I'm so glad you took the trouble to come here today, it really means a lot to me," he said, shaking each of their hands and kissing each on the cheek as he backed away. "I'm sorry to be so short, but they've got me on a tight schedule. We're on our way to Memphis where I'm due for another speech. Please Emma," he said in conclusion, "keep writing. I look forward to your letters."

Emma's feet didn't touch the ground as she floated back to Jackie's car. Jackie, equally enamored by the encounter, could barely contain her own excitement for the entire drive home.

The thrill of excitement they each received from seeing Rev. King again, however, became short lived. Two days after standing with him in the Valdosta City Hall, they sat in horror after turning on the nightly news, only to be informed Martin Luther King had been assassinated while standing on the balcony of the Lorraine Motel in Memphis. Emma and Jackie were inconsolable.

Through a flood of tears, Emma remarked, "First it was the president a few years ago, then his brother earlier this year, and now Reverend King. What in God's name has this country come to, Jackie."

"Pure evil, momma, plain and simple."

* * *

<u>South Georgia, 1970s:</u>

Many Americans were glad to see an end to one of the most tumultuous decades in our nation's history. 1960s America had become a time replete with civil unrest all across the land, due primarily to the racial divisions and bigotry against blacks which were still rampant in the South; and U.S. involvement in the Viet Nam War.

President Lyndon Johnson played a significant role in black American's struggle for equality, having signed the *Civil Rights Act of 1964,* and the *Voting Rights Act of 1965.* His presidency, however, was irreparably harmed by U.S. involvement in Viet Nam, compelling him to announce, prior to the presidential election of 1968, "I will not seek, nor will I accept, the nomination of my party for another term as president."

Although Tom Jr. received a college deferment from being drafted to serve in Viet Nam, he told his father he felt an obligation to follow in his father and grandfather's footsteps by serving his country in time of war.

"Concentrate on getting your education, and then we'll talk about it," Tom told his son. "Hopefully, this war will be over by then."

While the war had not officially ended by the time Tom Jr. finished his college education, the military draft had, and President Nixon had begun taking steps to end U.S. involvement in the war. Having watched for years the images on T.V. of U.S. soldiers fighting and dying in Viet Nam, Tom and Jackie felt relief their two sons would not have to go.

Like his older brother before him, Jim Franks had no desire to take over the family business, opting instead for a career in law. Following his graduation from high school in 1970, he enrolled at Emory University in Atlanta, where he planned on getting a bachelor's degree before moving on to law school. Inspired by the love of humanity he witnessed in his mother and grandmother, Jim wanted to become a lawyer and do what he could to help the underprivileged.

"Once I have my law degree, momma, I want to help people. I may even want to get involved with the legislature in Atlanta. With all due respect to daddy, I just don't see myself as a farmer."

"I know, sweetie," Jackie said, filled with pride as she looked into the eyes of her second son. "You can be anything you want to be, son. I'm already so proud of you. I mean, a peanut farmer just got elected governor, so I guess anything's possible," she added with a smile.

The peanut farmer to whom she referred, was Jimmy Carter, who campaigned on a pledge to end segregation. Emma and Jackie were thrilled to hear the words spoken by the governor-elect at his inauguration:

"The time of racial segregation is over…No poor, rural, weak, or black person should ever have to bear the additional burden of being deprived of the opportunity for an education, a job or simple justice."

"My goodness, Jackie, how sweet it is to hear something like that coming from our governor," Emma said, as she and Jackie watched the inaugural address on T.V.

"We're getting there, momma, we're getting there."

The words of encouragement from his mother were exactly what Jim needed to hear. His father, equally proud and supportive of Jim's desire to pursue a career other than farming, told his son to, "go be the best dad-gum lawyer you can be. The farm will survive without you," not too unlike the words spoken to Tom Jr. before he went off to college.

***

Much to their delight, Emma and Jackie had seen a significant decline in the number of intemperate comments and dirty looks from many of the neighbors over their heavy involvement in promoting racial unity in their tiny town of Morven. Although Brooks County schools were still segregated when the 1970s began, efforts were underway to end this segregation, something Emma and Jackie had been fighting for. They continued hosting community events where black and white children played together and spent untold hours volunteering their time to help educate children of color, disadvantaged for no other reason than being black.

With Tom Jr. and Jim away at college, and Karen in the midst of her senior year of high school, Jackie and Emma had much free time to devote themselves to some of the causes they had undertaken to help their world be a better place for those in need.

Perhaps harkening back to a time many years earlier when Emma tutored Old Man Jenkins' grandchildren in exchange for meat to serve her growing family, she enjoyed most of all seeing the look in a black child's eyes when he or she *got* something Emma was attempting to teach. The sheer delight of seeing a young child figure out a math problem, or understand some new concept, gave

Emma more happiness and satisfaction than she could imagine.

The weather in the fall of 1974 had become unusually crisp for that time of year in Morven. As the leaves began to change, beautiful shades of yellows and reds enveloped the countryside as Jackie and Emma got out of their car in one of Morven's predominantly black neighborhoods, there for yet another round of tutoring lessons.

"Be sure and keep your jacket zipped up, momma, there's a bit of a chill in the air," Jackie implored Emma, heading up the front walk of one house, while Jackie made her way to another.

"What would I do without you, darlin'," Emma replied, lovingly smiling back at Jackie, unmistakably the most precious and important person in her life. "I'm not sure I'd make it through the day unless you were looking out for me," she added sarcastically.

"You got it backwards; it's me who couldn't make it without you!" Jackie replied. "I love you, momma."

"I love you too, sweetie. Now go teach somebody how to read, I'll see ya in a little while."

Six-year-old Tessie burst out her front door when she saw Emma walking towards her.

"Hey Miss Emma!" the little girl squealed, always excited when these visits occurred. "Mom! Miss Emma's here!" she screamed through the door, letting her mother know their guest had arrived.

Wanda, Tessie's mom, had a fresh pitcher of sweet iced tea waiting, and poured Emma and her daughter a glass before the day's lesson began.

"I can't tell you how much it means to us, you stoppin' by and all, to help my Tessie," she said, handing Emma her glass of tea.

"Oh, I think I get more out of these lessons than you or Tessie," Emma said, taking a sip of tea and smiling lovingly at Tessie, before setting her glass down.

Wanda excused herself to the kitchen to get some fresh-baked bread she had made for her daughter and Emma to enjoy during their lesson. When she returned moments later, Tessie was standing beside Emma's chair, holding her hand and speaking to her, albeit with no response.

Emma, with her eyes open and looking forward, had a distant look on her face as she sat perfectly still in her chair.

"Miss Emma, Miss Emma," Wanda cried, gently shaking Emma's shoulders, trying to get a reaction.

None was forthcoming.

A sense of panic overcame Wanda as she continued to try and get a response from Emma, who remained still and unresponsive.

"Tessie, run across the street and get Miss Jackie. Tell her to come quick!"

Tessie did as her mother had instructed, and within minutes Jackie was at the side of her beloved mother-in-law, trying unsuccessfully as had Wanda, to elicit a response from Emma.

"Wanda, help me get her to my car," Jackie said, her voice cracking as she tried to suppress the wave of hysteria she suddenly felt.

After securing Emma in the back seat of the car, Tessie and her mom jumped in with her, as Jackie started the car and raced to the emergency room of the nearest hospital, located fifteen miles away in Valdosta.

Jackie, Wanda and Tessie prayed out loud for the entire trip, begging God to let Emma be okay. When their car screeched to a stop in front of the emergency room door, two hospital attendants ran outside to see how they could help.

"Please help my momma," Jackie pleaded to one of the attendants, as she cried uncontrollably.

Shaken and scared by the events she had witnessed, Wanda quietly prayed out loud, "Please dear Lord, don't let Miss Emma die. She means so much to me and my Tessie."

After watching Emma disappear behind a set of double doors, Jackie sat down alongside Wanda and Tessie in the waiting room, all three with their heads bowed in prayer, holding tightly to one another.

Jackie suddenly realized she needed to call Tom and let him know what had happened. At home feeding Bentley, whom they had *adopted* since Tom Jr.'s departure to college, Tom reacted relatively calmly to the news from Jackie.

"I'm on the way," he said to Jackie, as he grabbed his truck keys and bolted out the front door.

Driving furiously to the hospital to be beside his mother, Tom's mind drifted back to a previous trip to this very same hospital so many years earlier with his father. The thought could not escape him he may be losing his mother, as he had similarly lost his father so long ago.

Upon his arrival, Tom ran inside and found Jackie seated in the waiting room, sobbing with her face buried in the shoulder of her friend Wanda.

"I'm so scared Tom," she said through tears, standing up to embrace her husband.

Twenty minutes after Tom arrived at the hospital, Karen rushed into the waiting room and found her parents. After arriving home from school, she found the note left for her from her dad and hurried along to join them at the hospital. Her face became racked with fear as she approached the arms of her mother, silently praying to be met with good news.

"We're still waiting for the doctor to come out, honey," her mom told her. "We don't know anything right now."

"What happened, momma?" Karen asked.

"Grandma Emma had been over at Miss Wanda's house helping Tessie, and she seemed to suddenly go still. Tessie ran and got me, and when I got to her, she was staring off in the distance. Her eyes were open, and I kept talking to her, but she wouldn't respond."

Moments later, the double doors where Emma had disappeared behind opened, and the emergency room doctor appeared. After determining which of the loved ones in the waiting room belonged to Emma, he approached Tom and Jackie, wearing a very somber look.

"Are you Mrs. Franks' family?" the doctor asked.

"Yes," replied Tom. "I'm her son, and this is my wife Jackie and our daughter Karen. Wanda and Tessie are friends of my mother. They helped my wife get her to the hospital. What can you tell us?"

"I'm afraid your mother has had a massive stroke…" he began, only to be interrupted by Jackie's cry of anguish at hearing those words. "We have her sedated and on life-support. She is alive, but she suffered what's called a *hemorrhagic stroke.* She developed an aneurysm in one of the blood vessels in her brain, which eventually ruptured, causing excessive bleeding. We'll have a better idea in a day or two of what the prognosis is. Right now, we can only wait."

After thanking the doctor, Tom asked Karen to drive Wanda and Tessie back home, while he and her mother waited there.

When Wanda asked if there was anything more she could do, Tom answered, "right now, just pray."

"Oh, you know I will Mr. Tom. I love your momma more than you could know. She's as good a woman as God ever put on this earth, and can't nobody say otherwise."

"Thank you, Wanda," Tom replied. "And thank you for helping Jackie get her here. We are in your debt."

"Believe me, Mr. Tom," Wanda replied, squeezing both his and Jackie's hands, "Miss Emma done more for me than I could ever do for her. She's a saint, Mr. Tom, plain and simple. The world need more like her, and I just pray the good Lord ain't done using her yet. God bless you, and you too Miss Jackie."

Unfortunately, the news over the next couple of days did not improve. Despite the tremendous outpour of support and prayer from at least half of Morven, and other nearby towns, God had apparently concluded the work He had commissioned for Emma to perform.

After receiving the painful news Emma was effectively *brain dead,* Tom signed a hospital consent form indicating his desire to have her life-support machines turned off. While still heavily sedated so not to experience any discomfort, Emma slowly and quietly drifted away, breathing her last breaths with Tom and Jackie by her side.

As she looked into the face of the only mother she had ever known, through tears, Jackie quietly hummed one of Emma's favorite hymns, *Just a Closer Walk with Thee.*

***

The funeral service for Emma Whitaker Franks took place at Mt. Zion United Methodist Church in Morven, her home church for more than fifty years. At least half of the seats inside the church were occupied by members of Morven's black community, an acknowledgment of how much they meant to Emma, and how much she meant to them. With Wanda's help, Jackie arranged for the use of several school buses to facilitate the travel of many of those who lived in Wanda's neighborhood, who otherwise had no way of getting to the church.

An overflow crowd outside the church, easily three times the number of those inside, listened to the service on speakers, which had been set up outside to broadcast what was being said at the pulpit. A thick cloud cover kept the sun away, which would have been welcomed to those outside, many shivering from the cool air and occasional misting of rain. A price, however, they would all gladly have paid to show homage to perhaps the most beloved woman any of them had ever known.

Jackie wanted a choir to sing at Emma's service and again came to Wanda for help. Together, they tried to find as many of the young black children Emma had tutored over the years and asked them to form the choir. Although many were grown and since moved away, the choir still numbered nearly a hundred. No more fitting tribute could have been concocted to illustrate the impact one person had on the lives of so many. Morven, Georgia, had never seen the likes of Emma Franks before, and may well never see it again.

Cloudy for much of the day, Tom and Jackie worried about rain putting a damper on Emma's service. Except for a slight mist, the rain, quite fortunately, never came. Instead, as Emma's coffin slowly descended into its final resting place beside her beloved Eddie, the clouds above began to break, allowing bright rays of sunshine to illuminate the ground below. With her arm around Tom's waist, her head resting against his chest, Jackie's face began to beam, as she smiled and looked heavenwards, content in knowing it must've been Emma who had talked God into shining a light on all of them.

CHAPTER TWENTY-TWO

Happier Than a Pig in Slop

Within weeks of saying her final goodbye to Grandma Emma, it came time for Karen to report for freshman orientation at Emory University. It had been bad enough when Tom Jr. and Jimmy left home for school, but her only daughter and youngest child's departure became hard on Jackie to handle. With one more year of law school left at Emory, Jim was glad his little sister would be joining him on campus for his final year. Although he lived off campus in an apartment, while Karen would be staying in the freshman dorm, Jim figured to see his sister a lot over the coming year. As Jim helped his mom move Karen into her dorm room, he could see the transition of becoming an empty nester did not sit well with his mother.

Tom Jr. and Jim were exceptionally smart, but their little sister was clearly a notch above them. For years, Karen had told her mother and grandmother she wanted to become a pediatrician. Inspired by the way she saw her mother and Grandma Emma care for underprivileged children in and around their hometown, she yearned for the opportunity to do even more. Becoming a doctor and devoting her life to the care and welfare of children's health, is how she determined to accomplish this.

"It's pretty simple, dad," Karen told her father, when describing for him the path she needed to take to accomplish her goal. "First, I'll get my four-year degree. Then, four years of medical school, followed by a three-year residency in pediatrics. Eleven years in all. Piece of cake!"

"Good Lord, Karen, did you really come from my loins?" Tom said.

Laughing, Karen replied, "I must've got my smarts from momma."

"Yeah, you must've."

After making sure her daughter packed enough clothes, towels and sheets to get through her first semester of college, Jackie departed Atlanta and drove back down south to Morven. With Emma now gone, and all three of their children out of the house, Jackie worried about how quiet and lonely their home would now become for her and Tom. Before crossing the Brooks County line, she determined to begin talks with Tom about possibly moving.

"At least let's think about it, Tom," she said, not wanting him to feel like she was trying to push him into doing something against his will. "Earl and Bobby's boys are pretty much running things as it is, and we'd be close enough if you needed to get back down here. You'd only be three or four hours away."

Tom knew Emma's passing had been harder on Jackie than it had been on him or his two brothers. And with their three children now grown and gone, Tom would be willing to do anything to please his wife. Even after more than a quarter century of marriage, Tom still considered himself the luckiest man on God's green earth for having married Jackie in the first place.

Months earlier, Tom had a conversation with a local fertilizer distributor who had been thinking of buying a feed and fertilizer store in Newnan. Until now, such a venture would have been of no interest to Tom, but his priorities were in the process of changing.

He thought he'd give the gentleman a call to see if he went through with the deal.

"No, couldn't work it out, Tom," the man told him. "Honestly, I thought it was a pretty good deal. Still do. I just couldn't swing the financing. Why do you ask? You thinking of making an offer? I know it's still for sale."

"Well, let's just say I'd like to look into it. If the deal's as good as you say it is, it might be something I'm interested in."

Actually, the deal was better than his friend had suggested. Eager to sell so he could retire and move to Florida, the owner of the store jumped at Tom's cash offer, a full fifteen percent below asking.

Jackie became rapturous with delight when Tom told her the news. As much as she loved their home and town, nothing meant more to her than family. The thought of being only a few minutes' drive from each of her children was more than she could have hoped for.

"I don't deserve you, Tom Franks. You've made me so happy."

"It's what I do best, right darlin'?"

"Well, let's just say I got no complaints," she replied sarcastically, as she wrapped her arms around her husband and gave him a long kiss.

***

<u>Newnan, Georgia, 1976:</u>

With a population of less than twelve thousand, Newnan had the *small-town feel* Tom and Jackie had been accustomed to. Most of Coweta County had remained rural, with farming being the number one source of income for its inhabitants. Tom realized early on, if he properly ran his business, he could potentially be sitting on a proverbial gold mine. Like most things he tackled in life, he jumped in with both feet, finding new customers and building relationships with many in the farming community.

Jackie, meanwhile, continued the legacy passed along to her from Emma and became involved in a plethora of civic endeavors. Most days, she could be found volunteering at a local food bank, a crisis pregnancy center, or the Girl's and Boy's Club of Newnan. She also spearheaded the yearly clothes drive at Newnan First United Methodist Church, their new church home.

Already elated over their move to Newnan to be close to their children, Jackie became ecstatic when she found out she and Tom would become grandparents. Tom Jr. and his wife Rachel, who lived in nearby Peachtree City, invited Tom and Jackie over to their home for dinner where they announced the impending birth of their first child. Jackie didn't stop smiling for a week.

Karen regularly drove down to see her parents on most weekends, usually with stacks of books and papers in hand to keep on top of her studies. Although Jim's visits were fewer and farther between, Jackie understood, since he was one of the newer attorneys at his firm and had been required to work long hours. Nonetheless, Jackie had her family close, and with her first grand baby on the way, things could not be better.

"Thank you for giving me my children," she said to Tom, as they lay in bed one night. "I'm happier than I deserve."

"You know I hate to disagree with you, Jackie, but you deserve happiness more than anybody on this earth. I don't know where I'd be without you. Whatever I am, whatever I've done, it would all be meaningless without you. I still can't figure out what must've been going through your mind way back then; why you agreed to marry me in the first place."

Smiling, she reached over and poked Tom in the chest. "You looked cute with your shirt off, sweetie, it wasn't any more complicated than that."

***

The 1970s came and went without nearly the turmoil of the previous decade. Gone too, Jackie prayed, were silk shirts and disco music, affinities of her children's generation she could never understand. Although the country had been struggling through an economic recession, things were relatively calm, absent many of the incidents of racial unrest and anti-war protests, which came to define the 1960s. The peanut farmer who had become governor of Georgia, had become President of the United States, being challenged in his reelection bid in 1980 from a Hollywood actor.

Tom, as a member of the local Chamber of Commerce and chairman of the Coweta County Republican Party Association, was a staunch supporter of Ronald Reagan. Jackie, on the other hand, showing her independent side, supported the re-election of Jimmy Carter. Although divided politically with his wife, Tom had enough good sense not to rub it in when Reagan won in a landslide.

***

After ten years of hard work, including too many fifteen-hour days for Jim to count, he deservedly received a promotion to junior partner. The general partner of his law firm had always been supportive of Jim's desire to do *pro-bono* work on behalf of indigent clients, an onus he felt an obligation to perform, due primarily to the legacy imparted on him by his mother and grandmother. It was in this vein he went to his bosses for permission to take on a case he felt deserved the competency of his representation, and the resources of his firm.

Randall Dowdy was a forty-seven-year-old black man with a third-grade education, who made $15,000 a year as a janitor for an inner-city Atlanta public school. Latisha, his twelve-year-old daughter who attended the school where he worked, stopped by to see her father after the closing bell rang, before walking home from school. A walk of nearly a mile, Latisha had made this journey a hundred times in the past without incident.

On one particular afternoon, Latisha was confronted by a twenty-three-year-old white man named Billy Lee Collier, a known drug pusher and white supremacist from an upper-middle class home. Collier grabbed Latisha and pulled her into the woods, where he proceeded to rape the young girl, pounding his fist into her face and leaving her to die when he finished.

An hour later, Randall discovered his daughter's body, battered and bloodied, as he took the same path home after completing his day's work. After scooping her up, he rushed home and drove his daughter to the emergency room where she could be treated. Although her life had been saved, the savage rape and beating she suffered at the hands of Collier would scar her for the rest of her life.

Two days later, Atlanta police officers knocked on the front door of Collier's home and placed him under arrest for the assault.

A tip came into the police department from a man who overheard Collier bragging about the attack to some of his friends at a local bar. Subsequent to his arrest, Collier was afforded bail and released into the custody of his parents.

"I can't believe they let that no good *cracker* out on bail," Randall confided to a room full of teachers at the school where he worked. "He deserves to die for what he did to my baby."

The following day, Billy Lee Collier's body was found in an alleyway behind a convenience store, stuffed in the bottom of a large green dumpster. He had been shot in the head four times by an unhappy customer of his, upset Collier had ripped him off in a recent drug transaction. The murder weapon was never found.

When news of Collier's demise hit the papers, one of the teachers who heard Randall's comments regarding Billy Lee went to the police and told them what Randall had said. With the absence of any evidence to implicate anyone else, namely the guilty party, Randall was placed under arrest and charged with Billy Lee Collier's murder.

Jim Franks, who volunteered to represent Randall free of charge, went to visit him in jail after the judge handling the case refused Jim's request for his client to be released on bail.

"I didn't do it, Mr. Franks," Randall told his attorney. "I wanted to and probably would have if given the chance. But somebody beat me to it."

"First off, let's keep that kind of talk to ourselves, Randall. You don't need to be saying things like that to anyone but me, do you understand?"

"Yes sir, I do. I'll keep my mouth shut from now on."

"I wish you had thought of that before, but what's done is done. The police have sworn testimony from three of the teachers who heard you say you wanted Billy Lee to die. Now, it doesn't mean you did it, but it certainly doesn't look good."

"Yeah, I know. But Mr. Franks, what he did to my baby, he got what he deserved."

"I'm not saying I disagree with you, Randall. But the state has an obligation to punish people who take the law into their own hands. And right now, they're looking at you."

"But like I said, Mr. Franks, I didn't do it."

"Well then, we need to find out who did. Or at least try to cast some doubt in a jury's mind about it being you."

Jim's firm hired a private investigator to dig up whatever dirt he could find on Billy Lee Collier during the months preceding the start of Randall's trial. Through *discovery,* Jim had the statements of the teachers who overheard Randall say Collier deserved to die for what he did; and he had copies of the medical reports from the hospital concerning Latisha's injuries. The hospital report provided the District Attorney with a motive for Randall to kill Collier, and his statement in front of the teachers indicated the likelihood he carried it out.

In figuring out his defense strategy for trial, Jim considered appealing to the jury's sense of right and wrong, counting on them to view Collier's murder as moral and just, based on his barbaric actions against a twelve-year-old girl. While he would never acknowledge his client killed Collier, this strategy would hinge on the jury's ability to *excuse* the murder, if, in fact, they believed Randall did it. To say the least, it was a risky strategy at best.

A new and better strategy emerged when the private investigator uncovered evidence and witnesses who were willing to testify as to Collier's involvement in the drug business, and his connection to White Nationalists.

Not only can we make him out to be a perverted rapist, but a drug dealing Klansman as well, he thought.

Having garnered national headlines, primarily because of the racial component involved, Randall's trial got underway in Atlanta, as cable news satellite trucks littered the front lawn of the courthouse. White Nationalists, exercising their First Amendment rights to *peaceably assemble,* gathered outside the courthouse carrying signs calling for Randall Dowdy's conviction, upset over what they viewed as empathy being displayed for a murderer, simply because he is black.

In the end, the District Attorney's case against Randall had been purely circumstantial, since he could not produce a murder weapon, or any direct evidence implicating Randall. Jim, attacking the character of Collier by highlighting his connection to drug dealers and racists, tried to create doubt in the minds of the jury of his client's guilt.

With no evidence to the contrary, his closing argument to the jury suggested they consider the possibility Mr. Collier had been killed as a result of being involved in nefarious activities, and could have easily been murdered by someone else, and not his client. His strategy apparently worked, as the jury returned a verdict of *Not Guilty* after less than four hours of deliberation.

CHAPTER TWENTY-THREE

Lord Willin' and the Creek Don't Rise

It was time to celebrate in the Franks household. Not only did Jim win a big case, with wall-to-wall national exposure, but Karen announced she had decided to move her pediatrics practice from downtown Atlanta to a new medical facility under construction in Newnan. Not to be outdone by his two younger siblings, Tom Jr. announced he secured for his firm the engineering contract for the massive build-up set to take place in preparation for the Summer Olympics to be held in Atlanta in 1996.

Looking on in admiration, Jackie stared up at the large family portrait hanging on the wall above their fireplace. Tom and Jackie sat in the middle of the frame, surrounded by Tom Jr. and Rachel; Jim and his wife Jeni; and Karen and Hal. At their feet sat their eight grandchildren: Ken, Joel and George, belonging to Tom Jr. and Rachel; Jake, Katherine and Lauren, belonging to Jim and Jeni; and Matt and Michelle, belonging to Karen and Hal.

"God has been so good to us, Tom," Jackie commented. "I think your mom would be proud if she could see this," she said, nodding at the portrait.

"She can, sweetheart. And she is, believe me."

***

The years to follow would be filled with happy times, sad times, and everything in between. Earl and Bobby passed away within a year of each other, leaving Tom the sole owner of the farm in Morven. Their children and grandchildren, he promised, could remain on the farm as long as they continued to run it, which they had been doing for some time, with Tom acting as their consultant.

The new millennium came and went uneventfully, despite the national furor over Y2K and all the potential problems associated with it.

Although officially retired, Tom stopped by his store almost every day, primarily to shake hands and converse with all of the customers he had befriended over the years. He had placed the store in the capable hands of Tom Jr., who had recently retired after nearly thirty years as a successful engineer. Jim, now a senior partner with his law firm, had become active in politics, and much to the chagrin of his mother, a prominent member of the Republican Party. To his father's delight he was considering a run for the state legislature. As Karen's medical practice continued to boom, she began spending a third of her workday providing free medical care to underprivileged and disadvantaged children in Coweta and Fayette counties.

"Grandma Emma would be so proud of you, sweetheart," Jackie told her daughter.

"She's why I do it, momma. I'm who I am because of you and her. I had the best role models of anyone in history," she concluded, bringing a smile to her mother's face.

***

Newnan, Georgia, 2004:

The Newnan Fitness Club on Jackson Street bustled every morning, filled with people trying to get in shape and get their blood flowing before beginning their day. Tom rarely generated much of a sweat, opting to spend time relaxing in the coffee bar, reading the morning paper, after a non-exhilarating session on the treadmill. On the contrary, Jackie took her workouts more seriously. Working with a personal trainer, she usually started off with some light weightlifting followed by twenty minutes on an elliptical machine, sometimes concluding with a session of water aerobics in the pool.

"Invigorating, Tom, you should try it," she would always say.

Lately, however, her workouts had become far less strenuous. She seemed to fatigue much sooner than before, prompting Tom to remind her she wasn't quite as young as she used to be.

Driving home from the gym one morning, Tom noticed Jackie did not appear to be feeling well.

"Did you overdo it again, honey?" he asked.

"Just a little tired, I think."

"You've been tired a lot lately. Are you feeling okay?"

"Oh, I'm fine Tom. Like you've told me a thousand times, I'm not as young as I used to be. I think I might have pulled a muscle or something. It feels a little tender in here," she said, patting her stomach area.

"Well, it wouldn't surprise me. You always seem to go at it a little too hard. Look at me, I'm hardly ever sore or out of breath."

"How are you going to get sore lifting a cup of coffee?" she replied with a laugh. "Let's go home so I can lie down and rest. I'll be fine after a little nap."

Jackie seemed to feel tired a lot more over the next several days, even sluggish at times. The pulled muscle she thought she felt in her abdomen became a constant irritating annoyance. Her appetite, normally healthy, had become nearly non-existent.

"I thought taking it easy for a while would fix me," she said to Tom. "Maybe I need to go see Dr. Humber. I might be coming down with the flu, or something."

After listening to Jackie describe her symptoms and how she had been feeling for the past several weeks, her doctor suggested she undergo a pelvic exam, a blood test and a *transvaginal ultrasound.*

"We want to be on the safe side, Jackie," Dr. Humber told her. "It's probably nothing, but I'll feel a lot better after we've done those tests."

A week later, Jackie sat in Dr. Humber's office to go over the results of her tests, with Tom seated beside her holding her hand.

It was hard for them not to notice the somber look on Dr. Humber's face as he opened Jackie's file and began to speak.

"I'm sorry to tell you this, Jackie, but I'm afraid you have cancer..."

He paused for a moment to let the word sink in, as the blood seemed to instantly drain from Tom and Jackie's face. As tears began forming in their eyes, Dr. Humber continued.

"You have what is known as *ovarian carcinoma*. The slight discomfort you have been feeling in your abdomen is the result of a tumor which has formed on your ovaries. When I did my examination of you last week, I took a tissue sample from the tumor and sent it off to be tested. The result of the biopsy shows it to be malignant."

Unable to speak, Jackie heard very little of what her doctor was saying after hearing the word *cancer.*

"Can't the tumor be removed, doctor?" Tom asked, his voice cracking as he squeezed his wife's hand, the realization beginning to sink in of the gravity of the situation.

"We can, Tom," the doctor responded, "but unfortunately the cancer has metastasized and has spread to other vital organs in Jackie's abdomen. She has what's known as *Stage IV cancer.* Removing the tumor itself will do nothing to correct this. I'm afraid to say, at this point, treatment is the only option."

Although her face didn't show it, Jackie had once again begun to absorb what Dr. Humber was now telling her and Tom.

"What kind of treatment, doctor?" Jackie asked, longing to hear something to give her a glimmer of hope, in an otherwise hopeless situation.

"Radiation and chemotherapy are the most common types of treatment. We can also add more protein to your diet and put you on some medications, which I think will help. But keep in mind, these things, at best, will only slow the spread."

"Dr. Humber," Tom interjected, "can you tell us what time frame we're looking at? Is there any way to gauge how long she's got?"

No longer blinking and barely breathing, Jackie remained stoic as she and Tom waited for an answer.

"My best guess is six months to a year. Perhaps a little longer with aggressive treatment." Turning his gaze in her direction, the doctor continued. "These treatments will have side-effects which are much more difficult to handle for someone of your age, Jackie, so I want you both to be aware of them before coming to a decision on what to do."

"Like what, doctor?" Tom asked.

"The most common side-effects will be nausea, loss of appetite, changes in the skin, like itching, peeling, blistering and the like. Probably hair loss. Fatigue and loss of energy will most certainly occur, as well."

Surprisingly, Jackie remained incredibly calm throughout the conversation with Dr. Humber. A calmness even Tom could not fathom. What he failed to comprehend at this very moment, understandable as it was due to the turmoil he felt, was his wife's faith in a higher being and how having such faith would sustain her through any crisis. She didn't spend a big portion of her life on her knees before an almighty God, seeing Him answer prayer after prayer, only to have her faith destroyed in this moment. Instead, she held to a Biblical promise found in the book of Philippians and etched into her very soul:

"Have no anxiety at all, but in everything, by prayer and petition, with thanksgiving, make your requests known to God. Then, the

*peace of God that surpasses all understanding, will guard your
hearts and minds in Christ Jesus."*

A promise Jackie had every expectation God would fulfill.

"And without these treatments, Dr. Humber, how long do you
think I have?"

"Hard to say, Jackie. Probably less than a year."

Tom and Jackie hugged Dr. Humber on the way out, ensuring him
they would get back to him with their decision on how to proceed.

After opening the car door for Jackie and helping her in, Tom
got behind the wheel and started the car.

"Take me to the river, Tom," Jackie said, putting her hand on
his and staring empathetically into his eyes, concerned over the
pain she knew he most certainly felt inside.

***

Named for an Indian word meaning *painted rocks*, the
Chattahoochee River originates at the base of the Blue Ridge
Mountains in northeast Georgia and flows south through the Atlanta
suburbs before merging with the Flint River in South Georgia. The
two rivers come together to form the Apalachicola River, which
eventually dumps itself into the Gulf of America.

Chattahoochee Bend State Park, about twenty-five miles west
of Newnan, has hosted many a Franks family picnic or camping
trip. Taking his children boating or fishing on the river, reminded

Tom of all the time spent with his brothers doing the same on their little river near their home in Morven.

"You can solve a lot of the world's problems sitting on the bank of a river with a cane pole in your hand," he used to tell Tom Jr., who never quite understood what his father meant until many years later.

Jackie loved going out on the river, just her and Tom, particularly early in the morning. Before the sun poked its head over the tops of the trees lining the river, its rays would penetrate the millions of tiny gaps in the trees, shooting laser-like beams of light, which reflected off the glass-like surface of the water. The early morning mist rising from the surface of the water, combined with the shards of sunlight, produced an iridescent effect, which seemed to beguile Jackie every time she saw it.

"Look at God's painting, Tom," she commented, the first time he took her out after dawn had broken.

Tom learned on their very first trip up the river, these little excursions were not opportunities for them to share conversation. Jackie liked to sit in the front of the boat, facing forward, hearing only the sound of Tom's oar gently breaking through the water's surface as he rowed, the murmur of the trees blowing in the wind, or the birds chirping away at the start of a new day. Occasionally, a group of mallards would disturb the stillness of the water by tiptoeing across its surface before splashing in, all to Jackie's delight.

Jackie never felt closer to God than when Tom took her out on the river. After getting the news from Dr. Humber, it became time for Jackie and God to have a little *sit-down.*

As Tom quietly rowed, Jackie sat motionless, admiring God's handiwork as she reflected on the abundant life He had given her. She neither yearned for pity, nor would accept it from anyone, including Tom, for the predicament she now found herself in.

I have been blessed more than any one person could ever deserve, she thought. *I choose to define my life by how I have lived, not by how I die. If the Good Lord wants to take me, then I'll go willingly.*

Jackie Franks stopped living for herself decades ago. Her life had been devoted to serving her family, her friends and neighbors, and above all else…her God.

"I refuse to leave this earth kicking and screaming, angry at life and angry at God, for having been dealt a bad hand," she quietly whispered to herself, "but happy, contented and grateful."

Exactly how Emma did, she thought, before turning around to tell Tom it was time to head back.

"I want to sit down with the kids as soon as possible," she said. "And I want them to know everything is going to be all right."

CHAPTER TWENTY-FOUR

American by Birth, Southern by the Grace of God

The eight-bedroom, six-bath rental home on Santa Rosa Beach in Florida comfortably slept all twenty-three members of the Franks family, enjoying what would probably be Jackie's last family vacation. Fifty yards of pristine, crystal-like white sand separated the home from the warm waters of the Gulf of America. Semi-reclined in an Adirondack chair facing the setting sun, her feet nestled in the warm sand, Jackie sipped a glass of sweet, iced tea as she watched some of her family tend to the sandcastle under construction beside her.

The oversized T-shirt Jackie wore bore the painted handprints of her eight grandchildren and three great grandchildren, a gift of devotion to *Granny Jackie.* The penetrating warmth of the sun felt good on her face, and the sight around her of the legacy she helped create warmed her heart even more. Her smile beamed as she watched Ava, Brayden and Clay, their three great grandchildren, pour small buckets of wet sand over her husband's body, as he lay at the edge of the surf, pretending to be asleep.

"Pop, wake up!" Clay yelled, he and his two cousins laughing uncontrollably as they continued to pile on the mud.

In dire need of this very respite, Jackie felt a little bit weaker each day, as the cancer inside her continued on its wanton path of destruction. Despite some opinions within her family to the contrary, Jackie decided against undergoing the aggressive forms of treatment she knew would only make her feel worse, and ultimately rob her of the irreplaceable moments she now experienced. In the end, everyone, especially Tom, supported her decision and did everything they could to make her last days on earth as happy as they could possibly be.

"I'm not frightened, Tom," Jackie said, as she and Tom admired the splendor of the view from their balcony, watching the moon beams dance across the tops of the water as the waves crashed into the shore. "I know I've thanked you a million times before," she continued, "but I can never thank you enough for giving me the life I've had. There's absolutely nothing about my life I would change, sweetheart, and I'm including everything we're going through now. I truly believe God has what's best in store for all of us, and I'm not about to second-guess Him on this one."

"I know, Jackie, and I believe it too, I guess. But is it okay to be just a little bit upset at God over this? I mean, I never thought for a second you would go before me. Not to sound disrespectful, but God's gonna have some explainin' to do when I get up there."

Jackie smiled.

"Of course, it's okay for you to be upset with God. I am too, at times. I'm pretty sure He's big enough, and understanding enough, to take it. But in the end, you know as well as I do, He's always going to do what's best for us. We must believe that. I do, at least."

"Well, of course, you're right. You always are," he added with a smile.

Her strength continued to ebb over the next few months, until she no longer could walk or stand without assistance. Jackie's body, ravaged by the unrelenting rage of her horrible disease, had been reduced to a mere eighty pounds. Each night, Tom cradled his wife in his arms and carried her to the bedroom, before tucking her in for the night. Karen, who had taken a leave of absence from her practice to help her father, stayed by her mother's side every minute of the day. The rest of the family stopped in as much as they could, fully aware each visit with Granny Jackie might very well be their last.

Each night in the weeks leading up to her passing, Jackie enjoyed listening to a recording of the hymn, *It is Well with My Soul*. Penned by hymnist Horatio Spafford, the song had been written at a time of unparalleled personal grief following the loss of his five children in two separate tragic events. The words had special meaning to Jackie in her hour of anguish:

> *When peace like a river, attendeth my way,*
>
> *When sorrow like sea billows roll;*
>
> *Whatever my lot, thou hast taught me to know,*
>
> *It is well, it is well with my soul*

Whenever it played, her family members present sang along, always bringing a smile to Jackie's face, as she closed her eyes and hummed along with them.

Before taking her final breath, which she did in her own bed with most of her family at her side, Tom leaned over and pressed his cheek against hers. For a brief moment, he whispered something in her ear, as tears flowed down his cheek and onto her face. Although no one in the room could hear what he said, nor would they ask, it was a touching moment which brought tears to the eyes of everyone in the room.

"She's with Grandma Emma now, and I betcha it was a pretty happy reunion," Tom said, smiling through his tears.

***

Much as it had been for Emma's funeral, Jackie's service produced an overflow crowd at Newnan First United Methodist Church. Having engendered the love of virtually everyone she encountered during her time spent in Newnan, Jackie Franks had become a most beloved and revered member of their community. The emotions on display at her funeral were testament to this.

Following the conclusion of her service, Tom and their children accompanied her casket on the drive to Morven, where her final resting place would be. Another service was held at Mt. Zion, giving those in South Georgia a chance to say their final goodbyes, as well, before laying her to rest in the company of so many other Franks who had gone before her.

As her body slowly descended into the ground, Tom looked at the empty plot beside her, where he would one day lay, almost longing for the occasion when he would join her. He wasn't anxious to die, and felt he had a lot yet to accomplish in carrying out the legacy he and his wife had begun. Simply put, he didn't fear death, and from this day forward would be ready, willing and able whenever the Lord saw fit to call him home. Each day going forward, he realized, was one day closer to being reunited with the love of his life.

***

For more than a decade following the passing of Granny Jackie, her family continued with their lives, enjoying many successes along the way. All the grandchildren were now grown, some with families of their own. With the best part of him gone, Tom had a void in his heart which could never be filled. He didn't, however, allow it to keep him from being the best father, grandfather and great grandfather he could be.

Besides sitting around his old feed store talking with old friends, he spent a lot of time at local ball fields watching his great grandchildren play soccer, baseball or whatever sport happened to be in season.

Karen hosted a huge bash for her father's ninetieth birthday celebration, as well as those to follow.

"The parties keep gettin' bigger, Karen," he told his daughter at his ninety-third birthday get-together. "I guess each time you have one, you're thinking it will be my last," he added with a laugh.

"Ten more at the most, daddy, and then you're on your own," she quipped.

***

Tom's ninety-third would, indeed, be his last. As he lay clinging to life in his hospital bed, his eyes, for a moment, began to flutter. A nurse, who had come in to change his I.V. bag, noticed her patient beginning to show signs of waking up and went to the waiting room to let his family know. Tom Jr. and Karen had been anxiously awaiting this moment, after holding vigil at the hospital for more than a week. They both rushed in to be beside their father.

As Karen leaned in for a closer look at her father's face, she suggested to Tom Jr. it may be time to give their brother Jim a call and let him know their daddy may be coming to, affording them perhaps the last chance any of them would have to speak to him.

***

When the recent presidential election was held, the state of Georgia proved to be fertile ground for the eventual winner, as the Republican candidate swamped his competition in the Peach State. As he liked to do, the new president took several opportunities the following year to hold campaign-style rallies in various states, some of which helped usher him into the White House. Georgia happened to be on his list for one such visit, and the president planned on using the occasion to bolster support for its Republican governor by publicly thanking him for all of the campaigning he did for him leading up to the general election, and the overall good job he had been doing as governor.

The T.V. in Pop's hotel room had been tuned to the Fox News Channel, broadcasting shots of the crowd inside Phillips Arena in Atlanta, where twenty thousand-plus were waiting on the arrival of the president and their governor.

"I think you're right, Karen. I'll give him a call," Tom Jr. said as he pulled his cellphone from his pocket.

"Hello, Governor Franks' office, may I help you?" came the response when Tom Jr.'s call was answered.

"Hey, Charlotte, it's Tom. Is he in?"

"Hi Tom, yeah, he is. Hold on a sec…Oh, how's your daddy?"

241

"Thanks for asking, Charlotte. It's why I called, actually. It looks like he's trying to wake up. The doctor says we're definitely running out of time, so this may be our last chance to speak to him. I hate to bother my brother, especially with all you guys are dealing with, but this is probably the last chance we're going to have."

"Oh, absolutely, Tom. Of course. Let me put you right through, and please give Rachel my best."

"Thanks, I will."

A few seconds later, Tom Jr.'s little brother came on the line.

"Hey Tom, what's happening? Any change?"

"I think this is it, Jim. Dad looks like he's starting to wake up. Karen and I are with him right now, and he's starting to move his eyes. The doctor said there'd be a good chance he might wake up and we'd be able to talk to him. I'm thinking this is that chance. I doubt there'll be another one, to be honest with you. I know you've got a lot on your plate, but…"

"I'm on my way, big brother," Jim interjected before Tom Jr. could finish his sentence. "Should be there in under an hour. Just tell Pop to sit tight until I get there."

"You got it, Jim. Try not to get a ticket, now…oh wait, I guess a State Trooper will be driving you," Tom Jr. said with a smile.

"Always the smart-aleck," Jim replied.

After hanging up with his brother, Governor Jim Franks pulled his cellphone from his pocket and dialed the number to the president's chief of staff, waiting backstage at Phillips Arena for the arrival of the President of the United States, and the start of the rally.

"Hey governor," the chief of staff said, after recognizing who the call was coming from. "I'm backstage now, waiting on the president. He should be here in about twenty minutes, or so. How far out are you?"

"That's what I'm calling about, General, I'm not going to make it," Jim replied. "Please give my apologies to the president, but I've got a more pressing issue right now. This may be the last chance I have to see my father alive, and I can't miss it for anything."

He grabbed his coat and raced out of his office, stopping for a moment in front of his secretary's desk to have her notify his security detail he would be outside momentarily.

Forty-five minutes later, as Jim pulled into the parking lot at Piedmont Newnan Hospital, flanked by a pair of marked Georgia State Patrol cars, the phone in his pocket rang.

"Hello, Jim Franks," he said into the mouthpiece.

"Hey Jim, it's the president," came the reply.

"Yes, Mr. President, how are you? Again, I'm sorry about having to bail on you at the last minute, but…"

"But nothing, Jim," the President of the United States said, before Georgia Governor Jim Franks could finish his sentence. "You did the right thing. You need to be with your dad right now, so don't you worry about anything going on here. I think I can handle this crowd without you," the president added with a laugh. "But seriously, Jim, your family is more important than anything going on here. You look after them and we'll talk soon. Please give them all my best."

"Thank you, Mr. President. I will."

THE END

ABOUT THE AUTHOR

David Coppage was born and raised in Miami, Florida. He obtained his bachelor's and master's degree in criminal justice from Troy University in Troy, Alabama, in 1981 and 1985 respectively. He then spent the next 33 years pursuing his passion in law enforcement.

After 5 years as a police officer for the Montgomery, Alabama police department, David became a Special Agent for the U.S. Customs Service in 1986. His federal law enforcement career began with him chasing drug smugglers off the southern coast of Florida, operating go-fast boats for Customs. He also worked money laundering cases and other financial crimes, as well as internal corruption cases as part of the Internal Affairs division.

After 16 years with Customs, David transferred to the newly created U.S. Federal Air Marshals Service, formed shortly after 9/11. Following 12 years of flying domestic and international missions as an Air Marshal, David retired in 2014.

His career is chronicled in his self-published memoir entitled, *They Paid Me For This? Stories From Over Three Decades in Law Enforcement.* He also authored a political thriller novel entitled *Barbaric Justice,* which received "Top 5 Finalist" honors in the 2018 Next Generation Indie Book Awards.

Although David grew up in Miami, his parents, grandparents and the majority of his ancestors were all from the Deep South. Many of the stories in *Sittin' In Amen Corner* come directly from recitations he heard over many decades from family members who grew up impoverished in the South, eking out a living farming tobacco, corn, peanuts and other crops.

First-hand accounts of what life was like in the South during much of the twentieth century make their way into this charming story of Southern tradition, heritage and pride.

davidcoppage1959@gmail.com